OCTOBER

Books by Richard B. Wright

Adultery
Clara Callan
The Age of Longing
Sunset Manor
Tourists
The Teacher's Daughter
Final Things
Farthing's Fortunes
In the Middle of a Life
The Weekend Man

OCTOBER

A NOVEL

RICHARD B.
WRIGHT

A Phyllis Bruce Book
HARPERCOLLINS PUBLISHERS LTD

October
© 2007 by R. B. W. Book Inc. All rights reserved.

A Phyllis Bruce Book, published by HarperCollins Publishers Ltd.

First Edition

HarperCollins books may be purchased for educational, business,
or sales promotional use through our Special Markets Department.

HarperCollins Publishers Ltd
2 Bloor Street East, 20th Floor
Toronto, Ontario, Canada
M4W 1A8

www.harpercollins.ca

Library and Archives Canada Cataloguing in Publication

Wright, Richard B., 1937–
October / Richard B. Wright.—1st ed.

"A Phyllis Bruce book."
ISBN-13: 978-0-00-200689-7
ISBN-10: 0-00-200689-8

I. Title.

PS8595.R6O28 2007 C813'.54 C2007-902799-7

HC 9 8 7 6 5 4 3 2 1

Printed and bound in the United States
Design by Sharon Kish

For Phyllis
and for
Christopher, Vicki, Sydney, Abigail
Andrew, Wendy, Gage, and Millie

with love

OCTOBER

I went to England to see my daughter. This was in October 2004. Susan had phoned the previous week with her dire news. A Friday noon hour and I was preparing lunch in my apartment in Toronto. Tuna and tomato salad. Herbal tea. An apple. Like many older people nowadays, I am taking better care of myself than in previous decades, adhering to a regimen of the privileged middle class: a sensible diet with fresh vegetables and fruit, a brisk daily walk, moderate intake of alcohol, though now and then I am apt to depart from the latter and get a little tight with too much wine at dinner. At such times I feel entitled to indulge myself; either that or at seventy-four I no longer give a damn. Perhaps these are one and the same.

Susan's phone call was unexpected. Nowadays we keep in touch mostly by e-mail. When she calls, it is usually on a Sunday morning, the afternoon for her in Oxfordshire, when she is catching up on paperwork or preparing her Monday morning talk to the girls. But this was a Friday and I thought I could hear faintly the shouts and cries of girls at their games. Perhaps Susan had a window open onto the playing fields. When she asked how I was, the tone of her voice immediately put me on guard. It was the same tone I might have heard many years ago when she believed she had disappointed me with some trivial setback, an easy goal allowed in a hockey match (she had been a goalkeeper), or a minor accident with the family car. Susan has never liked to see me unhappy. But she got to her point quickly as she always does.

"Dad, I got some bad news yesterday."

I hadn't the chance to say *Yes?* or *What is it, Susan?* before she said, "I've got cancer, Dad, and the oncologist says it's very aggressive. Just like Mom's, I'm afraid."

So there they were, the words I had feared since her mother's death twenty-two years ago. What did I say to Susan's words? Either "My God" or "Jesus Christ." Odd, isn't it, how we still rely on religious language to convey our horror at adversity. Nor was it hard to detect in my daughter's voice the anguish, the sense of miserable unfairness at the heart of such news, with its grim foretelling of the months ahead: the surgery and radiation, the chemotherapy with its degrading assaults on the body, the hair loss and nausea, the weakness, the pitying looks of friends and strangers alike. I knew those looks would be as hard for Susan to bear as anything else she might have to endure. And all this the more wrenching for having arrived at a time when her life seemed a decided triumph; after twenty years of teaching and stellar administrative work, she had finally a school of her own to run.

She had taken the job at Woolford Abbey at the beginning of January and was determined to revive the fortunes of an old school that over recent years had fallen into neglect. It was not an easy job reassuring parents whose faith in the school had wavered, or deciding who on the faculty was worth keeping, or calming those alumni who were fussing (Susan's term) over perceived changes to tradition under the new headmistress from Canada. She once told me that there is no more reactionary human on the planet than an alumnus of a two-hundred-year-old school. But I knew Susan would be equal to these tasks, a calm presence as able and ready to discuss the refinancing of a loan with banker types as to settle down a homesick thirteen-year-old on a Sunday night in the first week of term. There was a great deal of work to do at Woolford, but she was excited to be a part of it all. And now this.

On that Friday she told me how a month ago she had gone to the school doctor about a small lump in her armpit. With her family history, Susan has generally been on guard for signs of disease; she was in fact quite assiduous about self-examination. Still, she did admit that over the past year, with the move to the U.K. and its attendant busyness, the scores of people to meet, the new routines, she had not been as vigilant. Meanwhile the malignancy had begun, the cancer cells metastasizing from the primary tumour in her left breast that she had not felt. Like her mother, Susan is a heavy-breasted woman, and the breast tissue itself (she told me this later) is particularly dense, sometimes making mammogram results obscure and detection difficult. The initial mammogram had revealed nothing, but the under-arm lump was still worrisome to her, and so she had insisted on a second test. It was then that they located the tumour. Her mother died in 1982 at the age of fifty-four from an especially virulent form of the disease that had reduced her terribly. How could it not? Leah was a big woman, but in the end she was scarcely anything at all physically, a kind of spirit creature, pale and wraithlike on the bed. Her face seemed smaller, the skin tighter to the skull beneath; I remember the wisps of hair that were valiantly attempting a comeback after the chemo, their softness under my fingers. Like a baby's hair.

Susan told me that things were moving quickly. Dr. Patel wanted her to go in for surgery within two weeks. I don't know how they managed to arrange it so quickly, and I didn't ask. I was just grateful that professional people were now dealing with all this. Meanwhile Susan had to tell various people at the school, beginning with the vice-principal, a woman named Esther Vail, who had applied for Susan's position. At first Susan had expected her to be understandably disappointed and perhaps embittered at being passed over. An enemy within the ranks. In fact, however, Esther Vail had taken her defeat well and been surprisingly helpful over the past several months. Susan appeared to have won her over and they were now on the verge of genuine friendship. I was not surprised by this; my daughter has a way of attracting people to her side. I saw it throughout her years as a school prefect and team captain, as a department head and as a vice-principal. People go to her for advice and she always gives freely of her time. There is about her an unassuming likeableness that she inherited from her mother, a valuable gift that nicely covers a darker side of her nature, which comes, alas, from me.

All this radical and iniquitous change lay immediately ahead, and listening to her on that Friday noon hour I could only stare at the tuna and tomato salad I no longer wanted. Beyond my kitchen window, a sunlit fall day. A day for walking along leaf-strewn streets and rejoicing in life. Or so I'd thought a half hour before Susan's call. I asked her if she wanted me to tell her brother and sister-in-law, and she said, yes, of course. Get things out in the open. And what of her best friend, Sophie Wasserman? I asked. But she had already spoken to Sophie, and for a moment I was hurt that I had not been the first to know. Our absurd vanities. Our desperate need to believe that we are always foremost in our children's thoughts. And this helpless pandering to self-regard invades everything even at the worst moments in life. Anyway, yes, she wanted me to tell David and Brenda and the children. Susan didn't ask me to come to the U.K., but I badly wanted to and I said I would e-mail flight information as soon as possible. She thanked me. There seemed little more to say over the telephone. Pointless, really, to mutter the usual bromides about not worrying, things have a way of working out, and so on. We both knew perfectly well that things often have a way of not working out. As for signing off with *I love you, I love you too*, both Susan and I long ago decided—perhaps playfully, it's true, but decided nonetheless—that the old phrase has taken such a battering in the popular culture of the past fifty years that it has been virtually emptied of meaning.

From her childhood on, Susan and I have watched movies together, and as she grew older, we fell into the habit of commenting on everything from plot improbabilities to outlandish dialogue. These sardonic observations came naturally to both of us, and I know it used to irritate my wife how quickly Susan and I could be transported into our own world of banter, a world Leah couldn't enter, for she simply didn't understand the rules of the game. Neither, for that matter, does my son, David. Different wiring in the brain, I suppose. During her adolescence and for some years after, Susan abandoned all this as other interests rightfully took over. But following her mother's death, we found ourselves from time to time sharing our old pastime. I can remember an evening when she came by for dinner and stayed on to watch a television movie in which two people kept behaving badly towards each other, yet ending each fall from grace with their little declarations "I love you," "I love you too." As the movie went on, Susan and I unwittingly resumed a familiar routine.

"Do you really think she loves him?"

"Well, she said she did."

"Yes. Many times."

"So did he."

"Yes, but I wonder, then, why they keep doing such awful things to each other?"

"I don't know. Maybe because they love each other."

"We know they do too."

"Yes, we've heard them say so."

"Many times."

"You can never say it too many times."

"I wonder."

Nonsense of course, but we both enjoy this sort of thing, and I have come to believe that in an important way, such evenings have defined our relationship over the years as well as anything else that has transpired between us. It seems that we're both at home with disdain, an attitude that to others looks merely exclusive in a childish way. Poor Leah never understood our need to criticize what to her was not worth the bother. But to Susan and me, it has always been a meeting of minds, a comfortable stance from which to approach the world. Leah was correct in a way; there is a good deal of childish jeering in our attitude. But it has also provided us with an opportunity to declare in a small way our objections to triteness. So we both knew where we stood on the subject of love. It didn't need saying.

After her phone call, I got on to the airlines and managed finally to get a flight on British Airways on Saturday night. A first-class seat at ruinous cost, but all they had. Early Sunday morning Susan met me at Heathrow. She looked tired, but was still very much the tall, handsome middle-aged woman I had seen in July when she spent a couple of weeks in Toronto. Yet beneath it all, the surge of the outlaw cells was underway. Pointless to dwell on it, but almost impossible not to.

I spent the next few days with her in the principal's spacious and elegant Georgian house, set back among oak trees as old as the school itself. From my bedroom window, I could look across the quad and see the girls in their burgundy sweaters and grey kilts, en route to classes and labs. Now and then, a solitary figure, books to her chest, looking a bit downcast. Why? I wondered. A disappointing mark on a test? The sudden expulsion from a group? On the way to her room with a problem that would likely vanish within the hour, lucky girl. I was living in a female world, surrounded by young women, and older ones on staff. Apart from the maintenance people and the gardeners, there were only three or four men around; I had caught a glimpse of them in the faculty lounge and thought they looked like fairly insubstantial specimens.

During the day, I walked about the grounds, laid out, Susan told me, by the eighteenth-century landscape architect Capability Brown. I returned the smiles of the big, amiable English schoolgirls who had doubtless heard of me. News travels quickly in the monastic enclosure of a boarding school. I was Miss Hillyer's father. The headmistress's old man. Imagine that! He must be an age, wouldn't you say, Cynthia? Still, I felt entirely at ease walking along the hallways or watching them at their games. I have been around young people for most of my life. I've enjoyed their energy and enthusiasm and not much minded their uncertainty and moodiness. After thirty-two years of university life, I was not fazed by the estrogenic commotion in the air of Woolford Abbey. It was, after all, only student life, and student life has a constancy whether it is lived in Toronto or Karachi or Oxfordshire. I found a favourite spot to read, a corner chair in the Farloe Library, a beautiful, oak-panelled space, the gift of a Victorian industrialist's widow who had attended the school. Susan told me that when Mrs. Farloe died, she was buried with a copy of Alfred Tennyson's *In Memoriam*. Susan knew the story would interest me and it did. It was pleasing to know that Alfred T's poetry had meant so much to the old lady who was responsible for that quiet room where generations of girls have read and studied.

I stayed with Susan for four days and in the evenings we discussed many things, not all of them necessarily related to her illness, though of course it was always there, a goblin crouching in a darkened corner of the room, waiting to appear as the centre of attention. We talked about the breakdown of her brother's marriage and his newfound happiness with his young woman, Nikki. My son, however, has left behind a family in disarray, an embittered wife (though Brenda is getting over it), a beautiful and troubled seventeen-year-old daughter, and a twelve-year-old son, small for his age and unsure of himself. We talked too about Sophie Wasserman, who was coming for a visit over Christmas. I knew that Susan would be more comfortable with Sophie's visit than with mine. Sophie is a large, expansive soul, the ideal foil for Susan's darker nature, which is why I think they have been lifelong friends beginning in grade three at St. Hilda's School.

September 5, 1967. The date has remained fixed in my memory, for on that Tuesday afternoon Susan came home to tell us that she had found a new friend. "Her name is Sophie and I already love her." This announcement was delivered with such solemn confidence that Leah and I both laughed. But we had a terrible time placating our eight-year-old daughter, who had stormed upstairs to her room, convinced that we were making fun of her. I suppose when all is said and done, Susan has spent more time in Sophie's company than in anyone else's. They have studied together, worried about teachers and boys, struggled through romances and Sophie's marriage to a terribly inept man. Sophie, I knew, would be the perfect person to be with Susan at this time.

All this we discussed, always circulating around the larger problem. The *only* problem if it came to that. I wanted to ask the awful question of how much time the medical people had talked about. Dr. Patel, Susan said, had been vague about details. It was hard to tell at this stage. Perhaps after the surgery she could be more specific. But all this uncertainty was perplexing. Should she carry on at the school after the surgery? She and Sophie had talked of returning to Toronto. Sophie said Susan could stay with her until she sorted out things. It was all dizzying, this speculation, and I could tell that Susan was easily irritated with me and my questions, and characteristically felt bad for being irritated with me. We both drank a bit too much on those evenings and I imagined the creature in the dark corner grinning hideously at us. Still, I felt that Susan was holding back. Not telling me the entire truth about her disease. I didn't want to press too hard, but her reticence left me feeling uncomfortable, even at times slightly unwanted, as if my being there was a hindrance to her getting on with things.

Now and then she would frown at me, as if perhaps I was looking too hard for something in her face, some clue to the mystery of her condition. I know she found this scrutiny bothersome. When Susan was a child of six or seven, I would find myself staring at her, but in those days with wonder and gratitude. Was this beautiful little girl actually my daughter? But the intensity of my gaze would unsettle her and she would look up from her book, clearly provoked. Ask me why I was staring at her. I couldn't tell her what I was feeling at the time; she would only have dismissed my admiration in some way. I was just being silly, or didn't I know that it was rude to stare? All this delivered in a snippy tone that always amused me. I might say "A cat can look at the queen, can't he?" and though pleased, she would scoff at my remark. Even at that age Susan was adept at scoffing. I think I caught some of that in the looks she gave me now and then during our evening talks.

I don't know. Perhaps I'm exaggerating all this, but at the best of times Susan and I know that being together for too long produces a certain tension between us. We have never talked about this, merely recognized its onset and struggled in vain over the years to contain our tempers. This has nothing to do with love, but with the fact that we are too much alike to remain in perfect equanimity for long. With our similar temperaments, maintaining an emotional balance is, to say the least, tricky. At one time Leah was the mediator between us. Now there is no one, and sooner or later impatience sets in and a mild disagreement emerges, often over something quite trivial, a misunderstood remark, a perceived slight. This invariably leads to shifting moods; a sullenness infects the air, the unspoken wish for a walk alone or early bedtime with a book. It's just the way we are, and though we didn't quarrel during my visit, our time together at Woolford Abbey was a little taxing to both of us, I think.

So during the day while Susan was in her office or at meetings, I walked about the grounds or read in the library. At one o'clock, we met for dinner in the Great Hall, where she usually ate with the girls, moving from table to table until she had covered the entire school, at which time she would start over again. She told me that some of the older faculty disapproved of this, but that didn't particularly bother her. The students were delightful company and anxious to know more about Canada. A few had been on skiing holidays in Alberta or had visited relatives in British Columbia or Ontario. I saw a sea of young faces in that dining hall, faces of all colours from around the world. After the meal I would return to the principal's house, which was really big enough for a family of ten, and clearly Susan's presence had as yet made little or no imprint. The newly renovated kitchen still looked unused, though my daughter had been in the house since January. The gas cooker might have been just lifted from a box and fitted into its slot against the wall. The cleansing pad I touched in its little tray was dry and hard as a stone. Susan has never been much of a cook and she told me she ate most of her meals in the Hall. When she entertained, the catering was managed by the school's kitchen staff. Yet in the evenings, in spite of my protests, she prepared a light supper for us. After years of living alone I'm a fair cook, but she was having none of it; I was her guest and so she would set about making a simple dish, like an omelette. There is something peculiarly heartbreaking in watching someone you love at tasks she is not particularly suited for but that she insists on doing anyway because she wants to please you. So watching Susan, in jeans and an old St. Hilda's sweatshirt, opening cupboard doors and reaching for plates and a skillet, was painfully touching. And I couldn't help wondering how long the eggs had been in the refrigerator.

On the night before I was to leave—Wednesday night—Susan thought we should go out to a new French restaurant in the nearby village. So we did. Around us the local gentry were tucking into their salade niçoise and lamb provençale and the air was filled with the smell of good food and the sound of posh accents and laughter. Under normal circumstances, it would have been easy to enjoy the evening, and we did our best, though I don't know why we ordered such elaborate dishes; neither of us had much appetite, and soup or salad and a starter would have done for each of us. A better move on my part was the wine and that was just sheer luck. It was far from being the most expensive on their list, but it was very good, the kind of wine that left me feeling immensely grateful to people who could produce such quality at a price a retired professor could afford. I watched Susan looking at a pretty woman about her own age a few tables away, and wondered if she was thinking, why me and not her. She asked me then what I was reading these days and I told her. Susan managed a wry smile and said her bedtime reading now was "cancer memoirs."

"It must be a new genre," she said. "The bookstores have entire shelves devoted to them. They're in with the self-help and yoga stuff. Mostly written by peppy women from California who jog ten miles a day and belong to little groups who meet each week and talk about 'their brush with death.'" She took another sip of wine. "But you know, in every book that I've read, the cancer was detected early and cleared up. So, they all have happy endings, at least for the time being." She looked briefly again at the pretty woman. "I don't imagine publishers are all that interested in stories about women whose cancer may be too far gone to respond to treatment. Like Mom's, for instance. And probably mine. Not peppy enough, I suppose." She seemed to take a deep breath. "Damn it, you just let your guard down once with this thing."

Her eyes brimmed then, and I reached across the table and squeezed her hand, my own tears not far away. I was thinking that all this was probably far more serious than Susan had let on, though I can't say that I was totally surprised. I was remembering her mother and the horrors she'd endured. But surely cancer treatment has improved in the past twenty years? I said.

"Yes and no," Susan replied matter-of-factly. "They still have to get it out of there, or somehow kill it, without killing you."

She finished her glass of wine looking cross and unconvinced—about everything under the sun, I imagined. I wanted to know exactly what the oncologist had told her.

"All right, I'll tell you," she said.

I remember how we were leaning into each other like conspirators. Whispering. Of course, no one was paying the slightest bit of attention to us. Why would they?

"Patel didn't say this in so many words, but I think she handed me a death sentence. I know that sounds dramatic, Dad, but it's true. Patel is very straightforward. I like her. I like her directness and her evident honesty. I'm paraphrasing here, but she said something along these lines: 'Let's not be under any illusions here, Miss Hillyer. You have a very aggressive cancer and unfortunately it has travelled to your lymph nodes. It requires immediate and radical treatment.' Then she asked me about family history and I told her about Mom. I also asked her if missing my annual checkup last fall could have made a difference, but she couldn't say. Or wouldn't. 'Cancer,' she said, 'can be wayward.' I remember that word *wayward*. 'Sometimes,' she said, 'we can accurately predict its course and sometimes not. It can go very quickly in any number of directions throughout the body or it can stay quiet for who knows how long.' I remember she was frowning as she told me all this and I got the distinct impression that cancer's unpredictability infuriated her. Made her smoulder with resentment. And it was all there under that impassive manner of hers. Well, you know doctors, Dad, you know how they always like to think they're in charge."

I had poured another glass of wine for her and she'd almost finished it.

"Anyway, I'm kicking myself now for not paying more attention. Damn it, I was going to see Halpern before I left Canada last December, but there was just so much to do. It seemed I was on the phone every day to people over here. Then there were all the parties and lunches to go to. Remember that lovely dinner party you and Brenda arranged for me. I enjoyed that."

"Yes, it was a wonderful evening."

"And Sophie was always taking me somewhere. She was going to miss me, I could tell. Anyway, I never did get to see Halpern. And then when I got here, I just soldiered on."

I told her not to be so hard on herself. She had picked up her knife and fork and was cutting her meat into small pieces. I asked about the possibility of another opinion, but Susan only shook her head.

"Dad, Patel is the best in Oxford, according to the school doctor. I have no good reason to doubt her."

Then she suddenly leaned forward again, almost knocking over her nearly empty glass, which I caught just in time. She was a little flushed with the wine.

"This thing," she whispered, "can go right into my lungs or bones. Maybe my brain. Isn't that a pleasant thought?"

"What can be done?" I asked.

She put down her knife and fork.

"They can remove my breast. Get rid of the primary tumour. Then they start with all that radiation and chemotherapy. You know those big wide hats or toques or turbans. Remember Mom with hers? She used to say she looked like one of those women who worked in factories in England during the war. Mom took it all so well."

"Not always," I said. But she didn't hear me.

"The thing is, Dad, I think it's a grass fire inside me. And the big question according to Patel is whether we can arrest it. The verb, incidentally, is hers. *Arrest*. As if the cancer is a thief stealing all my healthy cells. Whatever you choose to call it, it's in there ravaging away. God, I'm mixing my metaphors, aren't I. Funny how the only way we can picture cancer is through metaphor. A grass fire. A sneak thief. A little ravaging fiend inside you. But however you want to picture the damn thing, it's on a rampage, the cells dividing and multiplying, consuming the healthy ones."

This was unbearable and I wanted to tell her to stop. But I had to be careful. I could see she was furious with every healthy person in that damn restaurant, including me. She was pressing the napkin to her eyes.

"We shouldn't have come here," she said. "It was a mistake. All this food. Look at it." She was frowning at her plate. "I've never understood how convicts on Death Row could eat those huge meals before their execution." She looked up at me with another bitter little smile. "When we were about thirteen, Sophie and I used to read those tabloids like *National Enquirer.*

We bought them at a convenience store after school. I always told the man they were for Mom."

We both smiled at that, at the incongruous image of Leah reading a tabloid.

"For a while, Sophie and I were both addicted to the sensational and the grotesque. Often there was a story about some poor guy in prison somewhere in Texas or Louisiana who was going to be poisoned or electrocuted, and how the night before, he had asked for some extraordinary meal. Pork chops and gravy with a side order of grits. Peach ice cream and two Cokes."

Just then, the waitress came by our table, a lovely young woman and fetching in her French getup, with the long apron over black pants and a white shirt. She looked distressed. Asked if there was something wrong with our dinners.

"Not really," Susan said. "Mine is excellent but I just haven't much appetite this evening. Perhaps you could take this away and bring me some coffee."

"Same for me," I said.

After the waitress left, I said that we must at least finish the wine.

"Good idea," Susan said, adding, "I've been wondering." She stopped.

"Yes? What have you been wondering, Susan?" We were again leaning into the table.

"I've been wondering about all this treatment ahead of me. All this stuff the doctor says is going to happen. I mean, what purpose is it supposed to serve? What would happen if I did nothing?"

"Nothing?"

"Yes. Just let things take their course. I haven't talked to Patel about this, but I was thinking last night. I couldn't sleep and so I lay there thinking, what really is the point of going through all that if I'm going to end up dead anyway, say, a year from now." She looked at her glass. "This wine is really quite wonderful, isn't it. I'm going to finish it even though I probably shouldn't. We could end up in a hedgerow tonight, Dad. Wouldn't that be something? Woolford's new headmistress charged with impaired driving after a mishap on Wednesday evening just outside the village." She paused. "You see if I go through with all that stuff, it will probably mean I'll be a patient for the rest of my life. The chemotherapy sessions, the vomiting into bed-pans, the sitting around with other ravaged souls. All of us shrinking, disappearing in front of our visitors. I'm sorry, but I'm just trying to think all this through. It seems to me you consign your life to the care of others and so there you lie, sick as a dog most of the time."

"But, Susan, without all that, you'll surely grow weaker and sicker."

She shrugged as the waitress brought our coffee. "Maybe. I guess so."

I was trying to look at things from her viewpoint. She had watched her mother suffer through those debilitating routines that had given her a few more months but that in the end couldn't save her. So I could see Susan's point, but I was also surprised by her thinking. Our primal instinct is to survive, and of all people, Susan seemed to me an example of that instinct in action. She has never been one to give up anything without a fight. So it was uncharacteristic to hear her talking like this, and I put it down to the understandable depression that accompanied such news. It was natural to feel this way at first, but then most people begin to think of ways to fight the disease.

"I haven't said this to anyone except you," she said, "but I'm just wondering how long I could carry on and try to lead as normal a life as possible under these circumstances. I'll have to give up the school, of course. I'm going to tell Esther tomorrow. I think she already suspects something is not quite right, but like any good, civilized Englishwoman, she doesn't pry into the personal. I suppose I'll go back to Toronto."

"You can stay with me of course."

"No, Dad. I'm not going to burden you with all that. I may be close by, but I don't want to be under your roof. It wouldn't work. You know that."

I knew it, though I didn't like to hear it stated so emphatically.

"Sophie and I have talked about this," Susan said. "A little, anyway. She phoned back on Saturday because all I did when I first called her was bawl. So she phoned me back the next day and said she had some ideas. And she has the room. It might work, though I hate the idea of hanging around her place like that. I didn't mention the notion of just letting nature take its course. Sophie will be expecting me to go through all the hoops. You know Sophie."

"Yes," I said. "I know Sophie, and I know you too. This is not like you at all. Giving up without a fight." The wrong choice of words. Stupid, stupid, stupid—and so a flash of temper.

"I'm still just thinking this through, Dad. Okay? I only got the damn news six days ago and it takes some getting used to." We didn't speak for a few moments and then she said, "Let's get out of here."

The school was a couple of miles from the village and Susan drove carefully. Neither of us said anything as we watched the curving grey road unfold in the headlights. I noticed a hare pausing by the roadside as we passed. At the school Susan suggested a walk before turning in. It was only nine o'clock and the lights were still on in the dormitories. We could hear singing from the chapel. Choir practice.

> For all the saints who from their labours rest,
> Who thee by faith before the world confessed,
> Thy name, O Jesu, be for ever blest,
> Alleluia! Alleluia!

I had sung this hymn as a schoolboy at Groveland sixty years ago. Written by William Walsham How, the Bishop of Wakefield, infamous for having burned a copy of *Jude the Obscure* and discouraging Hardy from writing any more novels. This is the sort of useless information I carry around in my head after a lifetime with the Victorians. I was listening attentively to the choir, willing them to get it right. There's a tricky bit in the *Alleluia* and the girls were having trouble. The choirmaster kept stopping them and then they would have another go at it. So as we walked, we listened to the interrupted refrain as it came across the fields from behind the lighted windows of the chapel.

Eventually we stopped and sat on a bench from where we could look across at the school buildings. We sat in silence for a few moments, each of us trying to find a way back into conversation, though maybe Susan was simply admiring the quiet dark beauty of her surroundings. She has always been conscious of place and her favourite place has always been a garden. As a child she loved them. Her favourite book was *The Secret Garden*, and I used to read it to her, a chapter each night at bedtime. All her life she has worked in old buildings among green spaces. Schools like St. Hilda's and Woolford Abbey are really large gardens, aesthetically pleasing, a refuge from the hateful clamour and unsightliness of towns and cities. So perhaps on that Wednesday evening she was reflecting on what she would soon have to relinquish.

Then, quite unexpectedly she said, "Let me tell you about last Thursday, Dad. My terrible Thursday. A sunny day. A marvellous bright morning. Fresh smelling. There's almost no pollution here. At least I don't notice any. Not after Toronto. I was in my office and I had a phone call from Dr. Patel's secretary. Nine-thirty exactly. I remember because Esther was there for a meeting about a new teacher who was having problems. We'd been talking about this young woman and agreed that she would probably work out in time. The young woman was my first hiring and so I wanted her to succeed, and Esther realized that and wanted to do all she could to help. I admire that about her. Not a trace of spite. I think I told you that she wanted my job but was passed over, and so you could hardly blame her if she felt a little resentful. But no, we get along remarkably well. So there we were and we were coming up with a plan to help this young teacher. I'd had the biopsy three weeks before and it was always somewhere in the back of my mind, but you know how easy it is to get caught up in other things going on in your life. And then the phone call. The secretary said the doctor wanted to see me that afternoon, and I remember thinking, this can't be good. Good news can be conveyed over the telephone. But a face-to-face meeting on short notice? That can only be bad news. So I told the secretary, yes, I could be there at four. I was looking across at Esther, who was trying not to stare, though I sensed she knew that something serious was going on. Anyway, we finished our little meeting and I carried on with my day, my terrible Thursday. And all the time I was preparing myself. Driving into Oxford I kept thinking about Mom and what she went through. Yet when Patel actually told me, I was almost dizzy with disbelief. I was quite overwhelmed by the reality of it all, half listening as Patel talked about scheduling for surgery and so on. Even though I had been half expecting something like it from the moment of that phone call, I was still shocked. It's the way our minds work, I suppose. So there I was at a quarter to five on a perfectly ordinary Thursday afternoon. Ordinary for other people, I mean. I looked at them as I left Patel's office. On their way home from work or just out shopping. Students on their way to tutorials at the colleges. I couldn't go back to the carpark. I felt too shaky to drive. I needed a cup of coffee or a drink. Walking along Cornmarket Street, I kept looking at people in a completely different way. Hardly seeing them but at the same time seeing them all too clearly, if you can understand that, Dad. I was envying them. Every one of them, even the panhandlers and the mad people.

I kept thinking, you aren't going to die within the next year—though some of them will, but they don't know that, do they. And that's the mercy of it. Of course we all know we're going to die one day, but it's not the same kind of knowing, is it."

"No," I said, "I don't expect it is."

"My mind was whirling with all these thoughts. I was looking for a place to sit down and have a drink. I had to collect myself because I was having a real panic attack there on Cornmarket Street. And right then, coming out of Waterstone's, a woman who recognized me. A round face. Bright glassy eyes like a little doll figure. Smiling up at me. Holding her parcels. I vaguely remembered her from a reception for the parents of new day students at the beginning of term, but for the life of me I couldn't remember her name. I had to stop and chat. There was no way around it. Standing there with this little round-faced woman with the bright eyes. She must have wondered why I looked so vacant. But after all, there's just so much you can hide. And how she carried on. Wasn't the reception nice? Everyone was so nice to her and her husband. She so enjoyed herself. And Tricia or Tessa or whatever the hell her daughter's name is was so happy at Woolford. She's met ever so many nice friends. She comes home from school every day and talks about the nice friends she's met. And the teachers are so nice too. And nice, nice, nice . . . and I stood there listening to her, smiling, I suppose, in some mechanical way, but not listening because I kept wanting to tell her to shut up, I was probably dying, and what I'd really like to do, Mrs. So-and-So, is find a place to sit down and think about the next six months and how I want to spend them because I've just come from the doctor's office. Actually she's an oncologist and she's just told me."

I took Susan's hand again. She was now having a good cry, and I had mine too. We wept together, wiping our eyes from time to time and looking across the fields. The singers had finally satisfied the choirmaster and the chapel was now in darkness.

The next morning we stood on the platform at the little railway station in Woolford waiting for the train to Oxford. I wanted to take a few hours to walk around the old city before catching an afternoon train to Paddington. Half a century ago, I spent two years of post-graduate life in Oxford toiling on my Victorians. I've been back a number of times since, but I never tire of retracing my steps around streets and colleges that don't appear to me to have changed all that much. Nor did it escape my notice that at my age this could well be my last look. Under a sprinkling of rain I said, "I'm afraid I haven't been much help, Sue." She stood back then and gave me a bit of a shake. She was glad, though, that the visit was over. I could see that.

"Just being here was a great help," she said. "What else can you do? I have to deal with this."

"That's true," I said.

"Thanks for coming over, Dad," she whispered. "We'll just

have to wait and see what Patel has in mind. Who knows? I may be lucky."

She had a meeting to attend and was anxious not to be late. My conscientious daughter. Even as a child she had to be punctual, and was often furious with playmates who promised and then failed to show up on time. So we parted, and I waited among the commuters with my copy of *The Guardian*. It was early, not quite eight, and I looked across the parking lot to where Susan had rolled down the window of her little red car. We waved goodbye to each other and she drove off to her meeting.

My return flight wasn't until Sunday, and my plan was to spend Friday and Saturday in London with some time in the Victoria and Albert, looking, as I have done so often before, at the artifacts of another age. I'd reserved a room at a favourite hotel, the Edward Lear on Seymour Street near Marble Arch. I chose it many years ago because Lear had been a friend of Tennyson's and had lived in those rooms. It's also modestly priced for that part of London, and on the placemats in the breakfast room are limericks and poems by one of the nineteenth century's most eccentric and likeable geniuses. While eating breakfast there, I am always reminded of how much my five-year-old daughter enjoyed listening to Lear's delightful nonsense.

Pussy said to the Owl, "You elegant fowl!
How charmingly sweet you sing!
O let us be married! Too long we have tarried:
But what shall we do for a ring?"

The hotel is also near Wimpole Street, where as a young man Tennyson used to stay with the Hallam family. I have always loved Mayfair. Far too rich for my blood, but I like to walk its streets, imagining Alfred in another century, strolling in Hyde Park, perhaps admiring or being appalled by the many wonders of his time on display at the Great Exhibition of 1851. Examining the steam-driven contraptions, peering at the levers and gears of a mighty new age. Poor Alfred was in awe of scientific materialism, though terrified too by what it all might mean for the life of the soul. I still love the big park and the wide streets, now transformed from Alfred's day by automobiles driven by the sons of Saudi Arabian oil princes and beautifully dressed women from Asia. It is now a kind of fairytale world and this gawking is enjoyable. At least it took my mind off cancer and chemotherapy. Around me people were getting on with their lives, and looking at them as I walked was helping me get through my day.

On Friday afternoon, then, I was walking down Park Lane, looking up from time to time at the grey light between the branches of the plane trees, the pallid look of an autumn sky in London when a shower is not far away, conscious of the mild soiled air with its smells of diesel exhaust and dog shit, my senses as fully engaged as they can be in a man of advanced years. At the same time I was measuring my own sadness against the transient euphoria of being in my favourite city, knowing full well but troubled nevertheless by the knowledge that all of it—the green expanse of parkland, the colourfully dressed Japanese women and their parcels, the dog shit—would still be there after Susan was gone. There too was the solid refined presence of The Dorchester with its doorman in his livery, a wonderful old-fashioned bit of dress-up nonsense from the age of house servants. He was standing at the hotel entrance overseeing the arrival of a large American car, watching a young man in a dark suit unfold a wheelchair. I too stopped to watch. When the young man finished, he leaned into the back seat, re-emerging a moment later with an elderly man in his arms whom he placed carefully into the wheelchair. But not without protest. The move had provoked either discomfort or a ruffling of composure, for I distinctly heard the old man's cry, "Easy, Adam, for crying out loud."

For crying out loud. Surely an expression from the dustbin of American slang. I'd not heard it in years. But there it was, in front of The Dorchester, uttered by that shrunken huddled figure in the wheelchair. Above him the young man was fussing with a scarf. I was only perhaps thirty feet away and I could see the older man's profile, still handsome in its frailty, the white hair abundant. But it was that expression from the 1940s and the querulous tone that had captured my attention. Could it possibly be? I wondered. Was this old fellow the time-transformed version of the boy whose wheelchair I had pushed around a village in Quebec sixty years ago? It seemed improbable, yet there he was and I was suddenly transfixed with certainty. The young man was now kneeling down to adjust something at the back of the chair, and people leaving the hotel were stepping around with sidelong glances and respectful smiles. Here was an old party being wheeled into the hotel. Probably someone important. Maybe famous. An aging tycoon perhaps, all wrapped up in his muffler. As

I approached him, I was absolutely convinced that it was indeed Gabriel Fontaine. At the same time, I wondered if it might be better merely to pass by unnoticed, acknowledging the strangeness of life but letting it go. I doubted whether Gabriel would even remember me and it could precipitate a scene. Who is this man in the shabby raincoat? Why is he pestering me? The doorman, frowning in his fancy get-up, saying, *Move along now, sir, please.* Six decades is a fearfully long time to remember anyone, let alone a person who was in your life for only eight weeks. Yet during that summer we had seen a great deal of each other. And of course there was Odette.

Stopping a few feet away I said, "Gabriel, is it really you?"

At that very moment, the young man decided to readjust the scarf around Gabriel's throat and for his trouble had his hand slapped. Well, Gabriel certainly hadn't changed in some particulars; in our days together he would never allow anyone to touch him. Except Odette. He was always fussy about making his own way in the world, bedevilled but not defeated by the polio that he had lived with for several years. He was inclined then to wrestle his way out of the wheelchair, holding on to whatever was handy, a railing, a newel post, dragging his ruined legs across the floor, looking absolutely tragic, his beautiful young face strained with exertion, the very image of youthful heroism. Was it any wonder that girls adored him? Perhaps it was the mention now of his first name, for after all, who in London would address him like that? In any case, he looked up at once, fixing me with the glare that I remembered so well when he was feeling impatient or out of sorts. A reptilian look now in that sallow face, and I imagined the old brain trying to fit together my words with the grey-haired man before him. So I spared him the tiresome questions.

"I think you must be Gabriel Fontaine," I said. "I saw you last on Labour Day weekend in 1944. In front of the St. Lawrence Hotel in Percé. You were returning to the States after spending the summer in Quebec. I'm afraid we didn't part on very good terms. It's James Hillyer."

A gleam of interest, and then he took my hand and grinned.

"It's James, isn't it?" he said. "You used to come to that hotel with your uncle. Yes, and you were madly in love with a girl."

"Yes," I said. "Odette."

"But she liked me," he said with a bark of laughter.

He was clearly delighted with the recollection, and I remembered how Gabriel liked to win at everything: knock rummy, cribbage, Chinese checkers, girls.

"How long ago was it?" he asked.

"Sixty years."

Gabriel shook his head. "Sixty years. Christ Almighty. The year before the war ended. We used to look for German submarines in the Gulf of St. Lawrence. I had a pair of binoculars."

"Yes, I remember that."

"We never saw any, though. But they were there all the same. I read about them years later. They were right there under our noses."

"Yes."

He had grasped my hand with both of his. Poor Gabriel. A beseeching look in his face. I could tell he was excited to see me.

"But this is wonderful," he said, grinning. "What are you doing in London, James? Do you live here?"

"No, I live in Toronto," I said. "I'm here on a personal matter."

But he was scarcely listening, rummaging in his mind, I suppose, for memories of us.

"Your name was Hiller or Miller. It's all coming back to me now."

"Hillyer," I said. "James Hillyer."

"Yes, of course. James Hillyer. How wonderful to see you again."

He was still holding on to my hand. "This is Adam, by the way," he said. "My keeper. He's a damn nuisance to have around, but he looks after me. Of course, that's what he's paid to do. And paid very well, I might add."

The young man shrugged with a faint smile. What else could he do? With his blond hair and pleasant open face, he looked very like the young newscaster played by William Hurt in a movie from the 1980s called *Broadcast News*, which oddly enough I had seen on television one sleepless night not long ago. Adam looked to be one of those Midwestern Americans with German or Swedish forebears; there was a guileless amiability to his manner and he struck me as the sort of young man who would stop his car on a highway in the middle of Wisconsin or Minnesota to assist some helpless traveller. Peel off his jacket and roll up his sleeves, settle down on his haunches to jack up the car and change the tire. And not take a dime for his trouble. I wondered why he was looking after an irritable old man and not chasing girls and a career.

"James, are you free this evening?" asked Gabriel. "Would you consider being my guest for dinner? Right here in this hotel. I can promise you a good meal. Adam says the steak is superb. I can't eat steak any more, but there's no reason why you can't enjoy it. You look hale enough."

He wouldn't let go of my hand and it was a little embarrassing there in front of the hotel. The doorman looked bemused by it all.

"It's such a treat to see you, James, after all those years." Gabriel said. "Please say you'll come to dinner with me."

I was touched by his helplessness and his evident yearning for company. Gabriel, it seemed, had turned into one of life's stereotypes, the lonely, rich old man. But in fact, from the moment he offered it, I had been thinking about his invitation to dinner. After my wife's death twenty years ago, I travelled as much as I could. Both my children were more or less settled in their own ways by then, and I badly wanted to get out of the house from time to time. And so I took every opportunity to attend conferences and symposia, spent summers visiting old friends, and over the years used up my ration of sabbaticals. But the part I didn't like about travelling by myself was eating dinner alone. Many people are perfectly at ease with their book or newspaper, oblivious to those around them. I have seen them in hotel restaurants and in the dining rooms of transatlantic liners. But alone I've always felt exposed in such places. Imagined others casting looks of pity my way, seeing a lonely old fellow with no friends. So the notion of a meal alone in Mayfair, like some character in an Anita Brookner novel, held no charms for me. Besides, I was curious about Gabriel. How had he fared over the sixty years since I last saw him in the back seat of a taxi in that little Quebec village? It was an easy decision.

"As it happens, Gabriel, I am free this evening and would be happy to join you."

"Wonderful," he said, finally releasing my hand.

It had started to rain, lightly at first and then much harder; we could hear it hissing under the tires of passing cars. People had unfolded umbrellas, or scattered to doorways holding newspapers and briefcases over their heads. Adam had again set about tucking that scarf around Gabriel's throat.

"It's getting a little chilly, sir," he said.

The innocent friendliness of that American voice in the damp English air—but the old man again brushed his hand away.

"Stop fussing over me, for Christ's sake." Gabriel looked at me. "Adam can't wait to get inside and phone his boyfriend back in the States. Tell him what a hard time he's having with the old bastard."

There was no sensible reply to such a remark and so we listened to the rain. Gabriel, I remembered, had a genuine gift for cruelty, and nothing in the passing years seemed to have changed that.

"Let's say seven in the Grill Room, James," he said. "I have to dine early these days. I go to bed early too. Just like a child. Sonny boy here tucks me in at nine o'clock sharp, don't you, pal."

Gabriel smiled at the young man and then at me. Helpless and still furious about being in that wheelchair after all these years.

"So," he said, "the Grill Room at seven. I'm looking forward to this evening, James, so don't disappoint me. A wonderful surprise seeing you here in London."

He was already pointing towards the hotel door, and in one swift motion the doorman had stepped back to open the way for them. Adam pushed the chair forward and as they passed, Gabriel gave me a jaunty little salute. Waiting for the cloudburst to let up, I was astonished at how easy it was to summon up the envy and malice—affection too, it must be admitted—that I had once felt towards Gabriel Fontaine. Standing there looking out at the street in the rain, I also reminded myself that for at least ten minutes I hadn't thought of Susan.

When I first saw Gabriel he was sixteen, an extravagantly handsome youth who might have passed for the younger brother of the matinee idol Tyrone Power. The dark hair, sleekly oiled in the fashion of the day, had a perfect parting. He was leaning forward, talking to a young couple who were on their honeymoon. Gabriel was saying something that made them laugh. I would soon discover that he was filled with salacious speculation about what they were really getting up to in their room at night. Gabriel was wearing pleated slacks, an open-necked white shirt and a sleeveless sweater on which was a pattern of little marching elephants. White and brown saddle shoes. I remember what he was wearing so exactly because I had seen clothes just like them on boys at Groveland School, and for reasons I can't explain, even to myself, I despised this preppy garb, popular among a certain class in the 1940s. A class, I should add, of which I myself was a member. This was on the veranda of the St. Lawrence Hotel in Percé, Quebec. A sunny afternoon in July 1944. The

American national holiday would be celebrated in the middle of the following week, and in honour of the event and to please American guests, the hotel staff had already raised the Stars and Stripes. It was flapping in the wind at the top of the flagpole that was surrounded by a little circle of whitewashed stones at the back of the hotel. The veranda overlooked the Gulf of St. Lawrence and Bonaventure Island. From there you could also see the famous Percé Rock jutting into the sea.

My uncle had told me earlier that the boy I was to meet that afternoon had polio and I was not to stare at his legs, an admonition that quietly infuriated me, for it was yet another example of how badly Uncle Chester misread me. At least in my estimation. I expected then to see someone pale and ravaged by the disease. Polio, I knew, could ruin your chances for a normal life, and it struck mostly people my age. It arrived in the season you most eagerly looked forward to, and you feared it from the first warm days of June until the cooler weather after Labour Day. Poliomyelitis cast its long shadow over the summers of my generation, for we knew it could strike anyone, low or high. The president of the United States had polio, and although he ran the most powerful country in the world, he had to do it from a wheelchair, and all his money and influence could never change that. For lesser mortals, polio could be devastating. Doctors could put you in a formidable-looking contraption called an Iron Lung where you lay gasping for breath. You shuddered at magazine pictures of this enormous metal cylinder with the head of a child protruding from one end. You imagined yourself in that thing. During the summer months, polio made my mother frantic with worry; she insisted that I wash my hands several times a day with Lifebuoy soap. From the beginning of July, I was not allowed near a public swimming pool. One of my classmates at Groveland had a younger brother with polio, and the child once came to the school with their parents; he was a puny little fellow who was twelve but looked only half that age in his wheelchair, his legs wrapped up in a robe. I remember watching him as he stared out at boys on the playing field and I imagined him gazing ahead at a lifetime of missing out on things that we all took for granted, like running after a ball. This is what I had expected to see in the boy Uncle Chester wanted me to meet, this American with his outlandishly theatrical name, Gabriel Fontaine. It sounded phony to me.

It was the beginning of my summer holidays, and much against my will, I was spending the next several weeks in a fishing village on the Gaspé coast with my exasperated and exasperating uncle. When I first met Gabriel, I had been staying with Uncle Chester only a week, but already we were tired of each other, he with my sullen withdrawal from everything around me, and I with his affected and supercilious manner. The truth is that from the time I was a small child, we had never been comfortable in each other's company. By that summer, I had transmogrified from the little boy my uncle remembered into a shy, gawky fourteen-year-old with too much straw-coloured hair springing from my rather large head. I had grown several inches over the previous few months and seemed always on the verge of tipping over. Or so I imagined at the time. My ungainliness, my sprawling about on the sofas and chairs and beds, seemed to annoy my uncle, who was fine boned and precise, tidy to the point of fussiness. I was, as he invariably introduced me to strangers, his lanky and languid nephew. To be fair to him, I must have been a difficult guest, sulking about the house, making it perfectly clear that I would prefer to be almost anywhere else. That summer, Uncle Chester was putting up with me as a favour to the family.

At the end of the school year my mother had taken ill. Not physically, but mentally. And so somebody had to look after me. My father was a busy man, an important man who spent most of his time in Ottawa working for Mackenzie King's Liberal government. In his telephone call to the school, Father told me that my mother's nerves had got the better of her. It was the kind of circumspect choice of words used in those days to describe ailments or setbacks that were perceived to be vaguely embarrassing to a family's reputation. But I could read between the lines. I had heard the expression "nervous breakdown" before. It had surfaced now and then in overheard conversations. Mental illness, I gathered, was somehow connected to a malfunction of the nervous system, and so I might hear my parents talking about some acquaintance who had suffered one of these "nervous breakdowns." I came to understand, however imperfectly, that the term signified a general collapse of the will, a retreat from the world into oneself. It seemed to happen mostly to women, though sometimes also to unconfident young men who suddenly returned home after failing in some spectacular way at university or on their first job. Then they lived more or less permanently with their parents, making occasional visits to an asylum for electro-shock treatments, an experience that struck me as mysterious and terrifying. Such a young man lived in the street next to ours, and I sometimes saw him standing by one of the upstairs windows of his parents' house. I was mildly frightened of that dark, haunted figure, looking down on those who passed on the street below. I wondered what it felt like to be filled with electricity and what the young man thought about all day behind the bedroom curtains.

That year—my first at Groveland School—I had finished grade nine. Groveland was seventy miles east of Toronto, a boarding school for five hundred boys in a hilly area surrounded by woods and farmland near a small town on the shores of Lake Ontario. My uncle had gone to the school and had returned to teach there for several years in the 1930s. He was still fondly remembered by many of the masters, who never tired of telling me what an amusing chap he had been. The masters at Groveland were proud to have known him, for he was now the author of a popular series of books for boys, a series dealing with the adventures of Billy Benson, who attended a school much like Groveland. In his various exploits, Billy foiled bank robbers, kidnappers, and Nazi spies. I detested the books, but I kept that to myself, for the masters were in awe of Chester Ames. After all, he had been one of them, an old boy and a colleague and now an author. Fancy that!

My father had attended a school like Groveland in England and my mother too had been privately educated. Father had built a successful career with a large accounting firm in Toronto, and when the war began, he was seconded by powerful friends in government to work for a new bureaucracy called the Wartime Prices and Trade Board, an agency established to

regulate the price of goods and oversee the rationing of everything from sugar to gasoline. It was said that my father and
others like him were paid only a dollar a year, and I was proud
when asked by other boys in the first days of school what my
father was doing in the war. Some of their fathers were in the
service, but my dollar-a-year dad, I told them, could also pass
muster as a contributor to the war effort. Besides, he was older
than other fathers and he had served with the British Army
in the First War and been decorated. As a favour to the headmaster, he came to the school once, just before Thanksgiving
break, and gave a talk in the chapel, recounting his experiences from thirty years earlier in Flanders, using words like
sacrifice, and *loyalty* and *service* to the British Empire. He was
impressive, standing at the lectern in his dark blue suit, the
gold watch chain dangling from the vest pocket, the clipped
and cultivated Home Counties accent. I imagine I was proud
of him. I know his little talk that day cemented my relationship with one or two boys and made my first term at school
easier. For that, at least, I was grateful.

His phone call about Mother's nerves came on the afternoon before Prize Day, and I was duly summoned to the headmaster's office, where he left me alone sitting on a chair by his
desk. His secretary, a kind elderly woman, had left a glass of
milk and a biscuit on the desk and I supposed they were meant
for me, so I drank the milk and ate the biscuit while I waited.
I remember how strange it felt to be sitting there by myself
in the headmaster's office while the life of the school was
going on around me. I recall having an almost overpowering
urge to sit in the headmaster's chair, but I was afraid he might

enter at any time and I would look ridiculous. My father was calling from Toronto. He had taken an early morning train from Ottawa and was at home with my mother's sister, Aunt Margery. He told me they wouldn't be able to come down for the ceremony the next day, so I might just as well take the train home by myself and he would meet me at Union Station. It was too bad, but that's the way things were at the moment.

I thought it was just as well. I was winning no prizes the next day. I had been shut out from even the most humble guerdon, Third Swimming Enthusiasm Certificate, say, or Most Improved Glockenspiel Player. I had excelled at nothing, was merely a jog-along B student with a sullen disposition, and no doubt a disappointment to my father. I don't know. We never talked much. I think he was far too busy with other matters, his job, his ill wife, his girlfriend in Ottawa—a revelation I wouldn't discover until years later when Aunt Margery told me. In any case, he was a distant man, J. T. Hillyer, at least with me, and with Mother too, I think. Kind in his own way, and generous in providing us with the comforts of life, sincere I'm sure in his concern for our welfare and happiness. But distant all the same. Perhaps it was his age, his many years of bachelorhood in the company of army friends in clubs and on squash courts. He may even have been constitutionally unsuited for married life. Such people, I believe, do exist. My own daughter, for example.

When Father talked to me that day, he told me that as a consequence of my mother's illness there would have to be changes in our summer plans. I didn't like the sound of that one bit and, to this day, I am ashamed to confess that the idea of any changes to my summer plans bothered me more than my mother's condition. I hadn't much enjoyed my first year at Groveland School, and I was looking forward to long afternoons in the house on Crescent Road reading Charles Dickens. I liked the heat and emptiness of our street in summertime, with neighbouring families away at cottages in Muskoka and Georgian Bay. And I believe that my lifelong interest in the Victorians began that year at Groveland when I read *A Christmas Carol* and *Oliver Twist* and in the final term, *Nicholas Nickleby*. I liked the way Dickens described the alleys and courtyards of London, the helter-skelter lives of street urchins, the coach rides on country roads, the comings and goings of people who lived a hundred years before I was born. I was looking forward to reading *Great Expectations* that summer, lying on my bed, looking up from time to time at the big trees beyond the window, watching the leaf shadows on the walls of my room. Quiet and alone at last. It sounded just right for the dreamy, rather lazy boy that I was at the time. So my father's warning about a change in plans set my teeth on edge. I was prepared to be surly and uncooperative, though in the end I knew that I wouldn't put up much of a fight.

All this happened a few days after the D-Day invasion and the papers were filled with news of the fighting in Normandy. Nearly everyone at Groveland was an avid reader of the newspapers. We were all caught up in the enormous narrative that was unfolding overseas, particularly in Europe. The Pacific War against the Japanese seemed like a remote and exotic struggle, though on Saturday afternoons in the local town's theatre, we cheered on the Americans in movies like *A Yank in the R.A.F.* or

Flying Tigers, huddled in a row, ignoring the spitballs thrown by local toughs who despised us. There were sermons in chapel by Dr. Wende and a moment of silence for those lost in battle, including now and then an old boy. The war touched us all in a personal way because it involved older brothers and cousins, uncles, boys who had played on the football and hockey teams only a few years before. Yet ordinary life goes on, insisting that it too be heard even in the midst of great public drama. People quarrel or have affairs, break down and take to their beds. Ordinary unhappiness never stops for wars. And so it was in our house. When I returned to its dark hallways under the big leafy trees, I returned to a house of shadows and whispers. My father and Aunt Margery could often be seen at the dining room table conferring in low voices, my father seated in his vest and trousers, head bent, listening to his sister-in-law's view of things. My aunt whispering, hugging her pale freckled arms as if the house were freezing. Meanwhile my mother lay upstairs with the curtains drawn. She'd gone to bed for the rest of the year.

Aunt Margery must have been about forty then. I have somewhere an old newspaper picture of her, a young woman in a flapper dress of the 1920s smiling at the camera with three other privileged young Torontonians on some long-ago festive evening. The St. Andrew's Ball or something like it. Aunt Margery was quite the looker in her day, but she must have been too choosy, and after a while all the eligible men were either picked over or had merely faded away into drunkenness and failure. Or perhaps she came to enjoy the idea of living alone. She was an independent and no-nonsense type of person and over the years she adopted a wryly humorous view of herself. She and another woman ran a small bookstore on Eglinton Avenue. Some years later there was a radio program called *Our Miss Brooks* in which Eve Arden played the role of a single woman, a wisecracking schoolteacher. Listening to her, I was always reminded of Aunt Margery.

My father paced about the house, anxious that things get settled. "Yes, yes, that's much the best idea, Margery. You'll see to it, won't you?" He could barely disguise his impatience to catch the next train for Ottawa. But first matters had to be sorted out. Plans made and order restored. He was good that way. He would never leave you in the lurch, as people used to say. Doctors had been summoned and money allocated for care. There would be a long period of recuperation. From overheard conversations that weekend, I put together bits and pieces of information. Likely my mother knew something about Father's affair in Ottawa. She must have sensed a change in him. Or perhaps there had been a clue. A smear of lipstick, a trace of perfume on a shirt. It's hard to be fastidious all the time, even for a man like my father. It would all come out in due course, but that summer everything was lost in a fog and the house was freighted with anxiety and uncertainty. It must surely have contributed to Mother's illness. How could it not? So there she was in a room upstairs, and not the master bedroom either, but a small room at the back of the house overlooking the garden with a little library of its own where she kept her books. There was a wingback chair under a lamp with a tasselled shade. This is where she read into the long quiet hours of each new day.

What then was to be done with me, the boy who had only wanted to come home, and if it came to that, do essentially what my mother was doing? Occupy another bed in the house with young Pip for company. I can't remember now, but I think I must have made some weak argument for doing just that, maybe pointing out that I could mow the lawn and take out the trash. Surely two women needed someone around to do chores like that. But my father wanted me away for the summer and my aunt, normally an ally, agreed with him. It was to be a strictly female household; there was a great deal for two sisters to talk about and it was no place for a fourteen-year-old boy. My place would be with Uncle Chester, who spent the summer months in his Quebec fishing village writing his dreadful Billy Benson novels. I had a conversation with my mother about this. Pale and composed in her chair, Mother looked up at me over her reading glasses and remarked on how much I had grown over the months at school. She told me to try to be patient with her brother. She was the only one in the household who seemed to understand that Uncle Chester and I were not a good match, but there was no way around that and, after all, it was only for a few weeks. To which I remember saying, "Well, no, not exactly, Mother. It will in fact be several weeks. Eight to be exact. Eight is not a number that you can describe as a few." All that to an ailing mother whom I dearly loved. How miserable we can be to our parents at that age! Some thirty years later I would get the same treatment from my son, David.

Uncle Chester met me at the village station in his corduroy trousers and white shirt, a sweater knotted at the throat and carelessly thrown over his shoulders. A lifelong bachelor, he was trim and tall for those times, perhaps five ten or eleven. His hair was thinning and as if to compensate for the loss, he had grown a small ginger-coloured moustache, an adornment he would keep for the rest of his life. I'm sure he was gay, one of the old-fashioned kind, in the closet, peeping out in admiration at youthful male beauty. The two of us filled his little Willys car, and after inquiring about Mother, he wanted to know all about Groveland. How many of the graduating class were going into the service? How had First Cricket fared? In his day, my uncle had been one of the school's best bowlers. He also wanted to know how old So-and-So was, referring to friends on the faculty with absurd nicknames like Topper or Pudge.

For years my uncle rented rooms in a large white house on the edge of the village. It was owned by Mrs. Moore, a widow in her sixties who wore a shapeless dress and long apron every day except Sunday, when she put on a dark blue dress and white gloves and shoes, and drove to the small English church west of the village in her old Essex. In the weeks ahead, I would enjoy watching this antique go down the lane, blue smoke sputtering from its tailpipe. I knew that Mrs. Moore, like everyone else, had to use her car sparingly because my father was rationing her gasoline in support of the war effort. In time Mrs. Moore would remind me that she was descended from the United Empire Loyalists who had fled the horrors of American republicanism, finding refuge in this outpost of British civilization among French-Canadian loggers and fishermen. Mrs. Moore didn't seem to like me any more than

Uncle Chester did. Perhaps he had poisoned her opinion of me before I arrived, though it's more likely that she just didn't relish the presence of a sulky boy underfoot. I sensed that my being in the house at all was merely a favour to my uncle, whom she was proud to have as a guest. As she told me more than once, he was an educated gentleman and cultivated. I would grow very tired of hearing that word, *cultivated,* over the summer.

The house was large and built on rising ground two hundred feet off a gravel highway that ran through the village and, in fact, right around the coast. A few poplar trees had been planted at the front of the house, and I liked the way the leaves displayed their silvery undersides when the wind changed and a storm was approaching. There was also the sea and the vast sky and the green mountains to the west. It all had a rugged grandeur, though at first I despaired of the weeks ahead. With the melodramatic imagination of a bookish fourteen-year-old, I saw myself like Nicholas Nickleby, alone and friendless at Dotheboys Hall, where the repugnant Squeers ruled.

I was given a room in the attic where I had to be careful bending around the slope of the roof lest I knock my head against the rafters. But the prisonlike simplicity appealed to me: the narrow cot and brown blanket, the dresser for my clothes, the little desk where I could put my Dickens and a small hardcover edition of *Selected Poems of Alfred Tennyson,* which on a whim I had stolen from Groveland School library. On the train I had started "The Lady of Shalott," something I cannot imagine anyone reading nowadays unless under academic compulsion.

On either side of the river lie
Long fields of barley and of rye,
That clothe the wold and meet the sky:
And thro' the field the road runs by
To many tower'd Camelot.

I remember my excitement on the train at detecting what I thought was a spelling mistake in the third line—*wold* for world. I saw myself writing the publisher in London, England, about this. Only fourteen and already a budding pedant, on course for a life of instruction and fault-finding. And wrong, as I discovered years later when I became more familiar with Tennyson's English landscape.

In no time at all, I grew accustomed to my attic room, a kind of aerie, isolated and spartan, a refuge from my uncle and the landlady where I would devote my summer to another age. The window overlooked the Gulf of St. Lawrence and I could see the famous Percé Rock and the whalelike shape of the big island famous for its seabirds. A different and more distant view from the one on the veranda of the St. Lawrence Hotel that I would see within the week. From my window, I could also look across a field to an unpainted house, grey from the years and weather. On that first day, even before I had unpacked my valise, I was drawn to the window by the cries of children and a persistent creaking sound that turned out to be a clothesline pulley in motion. On the little gallery at the front of the house a girl was taking in clothes, drawing the trousers and flannel shirts towards her and stuffing them into a hamper. The wind was blowing the girl's dark hair about her face and flattening the dress against her body. I could see the outline of her breasts. Sheer delicious torment to a boy in an age when the sight of a girl's breasts, even the outline of them, was rare and therefore precious.

Behind the house was a shed and a woodpile and an old car without wheels, which over the years had sunk into the grass, rusted and windowless. Several children were running about; a boy was trying to roll an old wheel with a stick, and a girl was pulling a smaller child in a wagon down the lane towards the gate. She was running, and the dust from the lane was stirred up and snatched away by the wind. How entirely clear is my recollection of the Huards' yard on that long-ago summer afternoon! I remember how at the gate the girl veered too quickly and the wagon overturned, spilling the child into the grass. He wailed at once and the girl picked him up and, labouring with his weight, carried him back towards the house. The others ran down the lane towards her, but the girl at the clothesline ignored the commotion, and after gathering the last sweater, settled the basket on her hip, opened the door, and disappeared into the house.

That was my first view of Odette, though I soon learned her weekly routine. Except for Mondays, she was away most of the time, and I assumed she worked somewhere. At seven o'clock in the morning, she walked down the lane to the gate. Resting my chin on the ledge of the window, I watched her through the screen. After a few minutes, an old Ford truck would stop and I could hear the voices speaking French, the quick run-together notes of another language coming across the field on the early morning air. There was another girl with the driver and often there was laughter as Odette climbed into the truck. I used to wonder how people could be so good-natured so early in the day. In the late afternoon, the truck returned and Odette got out and waved goodbye and walked up the lane, the children running to meet her and calling out, "Odette, Odette, Odette." A black-and-white dog ran down the lane too, barking with excitement. Like her family, I also looked forward to Odette's return, and after she went into the house nothing else was left in my day except dinner with my uncle and the long evening ahead. Like a prisoner, I would make a large X on the calendar signifying the day's passing. Before leaving the house on Crescent Road, I had, in a fit of pique, ripped July and August from the kitchen calendar, leaving, for my mother and aunt, a singular reminder of my banishment. The two pages of the calendar were now tacked to the wall above the desk, and filling in a blank space with a large X each day gave me a peculiar sense of accomplishment.

Looking back now I can see how utterly impossible I must have been, moping about the house where Mrs. Moore and I seemed constantly to be running into each other as we climbed or descended stairs, entered or left rooms. In the mornings, Uncle Chester worked, and so I was constrained to be quiet, passing his door on tiptoe. Mrs. Moore was in charge of maintaining peace and quiet, proud to have the author under her roof for another summer. But I couldn't bear the sound of the clattering typewriter, or worse, the sudden guffaw as my uncle invented yet another prank for Billy and his chums to inflict upon Headmaster Boyle. Perhaps I am being too hard on poor Chester. Not so long ago, I reread parts of one of his books, and really it wasn't that bad for its time and audience. I don't know how it managed to stay on my bookshelf all these years, but there it was with its faded blue binding, the dust cover long gone, its cheap rough paper with the black-and-white illustrations of wide-eyed boys behind a flashlight in a dark room, or a motorboat bearing huddled figures across a lake. Another adventure for Billy and his friends with help from Roberts the handyman, whose potting shed behind the hockey rink was a midnight meeting place. My copy was inscribed *For James from Uncle Chester. Christmas 1942.*

In the afternoons, my uncle drove to Percé, ten miles away, to play bridge with friends at the St. Lawrence Hotel. Mrs. Moore usually walked to the Robin, Jones & Whitman store or visited friends in the village, and I was free to wander about the house, inspecting the pictures on the walls of the parlour or gently lifting the lid of the old gramophone, which stood on a stand in one corner of the room. In his day, the widow's husband had been a mill owner and there was a photograph of working men in shirt sleeves with big moustaches standing in front of an enormous log pile, and Mr. Moore at the centre of the picture in his suit and derby. Perhaps an itinerant photographer had talked the old man into a photo shoot on a Saturday afternoon when the work was finished. The Boss and the Boys. There was a wedding picture too in which a young woman, who didn't look at all like Mrs. Moore but must have been, stood next to a young man, both staring into the eye of the camera. On the walls, the homely appeals to God for assistance and protection: *Bless This House O Lord We Pray / Keep It Safe By Night and Day.* I often entered my uncle's room too, peering into his closet, sniffing the tobacco smoke that lingered in the air, and now and then sticking one of his pipes in my mouth and striking poses by the mirror. The author at home. The author signing one of his books at the T. Eaton Company in Toronto. And always I sneered at the awful neatness of his quarters. A place for everything and everything in its place. A prefect's room after a junior boy had done the fagging. Uncle Chester had been a prefect at Groveland. Of course when I think of it now, I have to admit that my own room in the attic was not unlike my uncle's in its tidy arrangement of things.

After a week, my intractable sullenness, my orchestrated rudeness had clearly tried the patience of my keepers, and one evening after dinner, Uncle Chester revealed his plan. We were still at the dining room table, but we had finished Mrs. Moore's excellent fish pie and the stewed fruit and lemon loaf. The second cup of tea had been poured and my uncle had fired up one of his pipes.

"Well, what are you going to do with yourself this summer, James?"

He was leaning back in his chair, looking out the window at the afterglow of the sunset. The clouds over the mountains were ablaze with colour, majestic reds and golds. If you wanted a comforting image of the celestial city, there it was in the western sky. My uncle may have been admiring the view, but to me he looked exactly like one of those teachers who asked you a question, and then turned to the window as if to convey his deep weariness with the sloth and ignorance of the world, summed up by your very presence before him.

"You can't just sit around the house, you know. You'll be underfoot and in the way—will he not, Mrs. Moore?"

Mrs. Moore was clearing the dishes from the table and she nodded in agreement, as I had fully expected her to do.

"I would say so, Mr. Ames."

"Indeed," said Uncle Chester, "and it might come to pass that Mrs. Moore—with justification, I should add—might find it necessary to take the broom to you, sir. Am I correct, Mrs. Moore?"

"Absolutely, Mr. Ames."

During this bit of Dickensian tomfoolery I felt like laughing, but I didn't want to give my uncle the satisfaction of believing that I found him amusing. He was still staring out the window at the gorgeously coloured sky.

"Well," he said, "I think I may have the answer to our young friend's anomie, Mrs. Moore."

"That's good, Mr. Ames," she said, carrying a stack of soiled dishes into the kitchen.

I'm sure she didn't understand the meaning of the word *anomie,* but then neither did I, surmising only that it had something to do with my sloth and ignorance.

"A friend of mine has a son, James," said Uncle Chester, sitting up and looking at me, all business now. "He's a bit older than you. Sixteen, I think. Poor chap has polio. He could use some youthful companionship. I've talked to his mother about this and she agrees. You'll like him. Gabriel is a bright young man. Not the least bit intimidated by his handicap. Not a trace of self-pity. A truly admirable boy." He might have been dictating end-of-term comments for Gabriel Fontaine's report card. "I think you two will get along famously," he said, adding, "but try not to stare at his legs, James. He's understandably quite sensitive about that." As I've already mentioned, infuriating.

And so that was how I came to be on the veranda of the St. Lawrence Hotel in Percé, Quebec, on that July Saturday in 1944, watching Gabriel Fontaine lean forward and say something that made the young honeymooners laugh. I'm sure I must have been irritated by everything I saw before me that afternoon: the sound of laughter, the sight of well-to-do people being attended to by the French-Canadian waiters in their black trousers and white shirts. To me it all seemed too frivolous for words. Was there not a war going on? Had the Allies not landed in Normandy only a month before? The fate of the free world hung in the balance et cetera, et cetera. And here were these people carrying on as if nothing crucial was taking place at all. Talking and laughing at the very moment when Nazi submarines could be sliding under the water that we looked out upon. Just exactly what I expected those people to do about it I didn't know, but their levity seemed wrong somehow. I don't think, however, that my stance of the sober-faced young killjoy fazed anyone.

Uncle Chester introduced me to Mrs. Fontaine and to the Porters, a wealthy couple from Boston who pronounced their vowels in an odd way. Or so it seemed to me.

They were all sitting in big maple chairs on the veranda and they waved to us as we approached, Mrs. Fontaine calling out, "Here you are at last, you naughty man. We've been waiting ages."

Mrs. Porter said, "Chestah, I'd have been scared to death driving that little ca' through those hills."

"And is this your nephew, then?" asked Mrs. Fontaine.

"Yes," said Uncle Chester. "This is my lanky and languid nephew James."

"What a handsome young man," said Mrs. Fontaine.

I knew she was lying. I wasn't handsome at all. I knew what I was, an ungainly towheaded boy who had grown several inches in the past few months and was still uncomfortable with his new body, bruising his shins on low tables and unaccountably dropping things, affecting a sullen manner that he hoped would be taken for gravitas. But gauche as I was, I could see even then that my uncle and Mrs. Fontaine were engaged in an elaborate game of amusing each other by excluding others; their language and deportment were often extravagant and theatrical, and what it all amounted to, I thought, was a barely concealed contempt for most of their fellow humans. A younger Mrs. Fontaine must have been a spectacular beauty and she still had the bearing of someone accustomed to admiration. She was then in her early forties with luminous fair skin, light brown hair, and dark eyes. She was wearing a white shirt with a colourful scarf tucked around her throat and those wide slacks that were popular with women during the war years. In the trousers and shirt she exhibited a crisp masculine beauty that day, something exotic and glamorous that reminded me of no less a figure than Wallis Simpson, the American divorcee who had beguiled a king and transformed him into a mere duke. Her picture could often be seen in *Life* and other popular magazines.

I was looking around expecting to see someone fragile and small, withering away in a chair like the brother of my Groveland classmate. So I was startled when Mrs. Fontaine called out to the good-looking boy at the far end of the veranda who was talking to the young couple. I hadn't seen the wheelchair. Rising slowly, he waved and began to make his way towards us. Others parted to let him pass. With the help of two canes, he set forth, and I wondered why he was doing this. Why was he putting himself through the humiliation of showing us just what a punishing ordeal it was simply to move across a crowded floor? I felt embarrassed for him, but as usual I misread the whole thing. Gabriel was leaning on his canes, dragging his feet onward in a tortured effortful lurch, but grinning all the same, and I think I caught something in his wicked leer that said, *Have a good gawk, you bastards.* Still, I felt he might topple at any moment, and what then? Would others rush forward to help and would he curse them, scrambling about on the floor for his sticks? What he was doing you could imagine a polio patient enduring in a gymnasium, with a trainer at the other end of the parallel bars urging him on but not especially dismayed should he fall. But there on the veranda? It seemed like such a bravura performance. Not a hair on his sleek head was out of place as he dragged those brown and white saddle shoes across the floor. Tyrone Power's cocky kid brother. He made it, too, panting a little from his exertions. His mother touched his arm lightly, almost diffidently.

"Gabriel, this is Chester's nephew, James. He's visiting for the summer too. I know you're going to be the best of friends."

"How on earth would you know such a thing, Mother?" asked Gabriel, smiling at me as he fussed with his canes, freeing a hand to shake mine.

It was a marvellous put-down, I thought.

Mrs. Fontaine smiled. "I just know, dear."

I was taller than Gabriel, and despite his handsomeness, I could see that the disease had done its work. Up close he looked shrunken. A little stoop in his shoulders. The grin seemed willed. His first words to me were framed as a sarcastic question.

"How about taking me for a spin, James? Mother, can you have one of these chaps fetch the carriage?" He gave a very good imitation of the English actor Ronald Colman and was already laughing at his little joke.

But what was it all about? A spin? The carriage? I felt I was being mocked. A waiter, however, was summoned to bring his wheelchair, and Gabriel settled into it, looking up at me pleasantly.

"We have to go through the lobby, old boy," he said. "Give everyone a chance to see the cripple. It makes them happy. *Schadenfreude* and all that."

I didn't know what the word meant but it sounded German, and adamant young patriot that I was, I didn't like it. Nor did I much like the idea of playing servant to this rich American smart aleck with his preppy clothes and phony accent. I was already halfway to hating my uncle for his solution to my "sloth" and "anomie." Mrs. F had abruptly left us, joining the others, who were anxious to begin their bridge game. Through a window I could see the Porters sitting around a table in the lounge with Uncle Chester, who was shuffling the cards.

Gabriel was right. People did stare. But not only because he was crippled. He was wrong about that. They stared because they saw a beautiful young man in a ruined body. We are intrigued by the vagaries of fortune, how good luck and bad are often conjoined. How then could people help gaping at a boy who had looks and money, but who faced a slow-motion journey through life, entirely dependent on servants or the goodwill of plain fellows like myself. So I pushed him through the hotel lobby to the front entrance. This was long before public buildings provided ramps for the handicapped—those afflicted had to make do with what was there—and the hotel had placed two planks at one end of the veranda, so that the heavy wooden chair could be manoeuvred down to the grass and onto the front walk. On the village street, pretty girls in their skirts and blouses stepped aside to let us pass, smiling at the young prince, but with scarcely a glance my way. Looking down at Gabriel's shoulders and the dark hair with its perfect parting, I silently cursed my own springy mop, dry as hay. The things that torment us when we are young.

Gabriel talked about his father, a professor of economics who was working in Washington even though he was a Republican and despised most of the New Deal people there. I got the impression that Professor Fontaine was much older than his beautiful wife. I thought it was an interesting coincidence that my father also worked for the government, and I muttered something about J. T. Hillyer, the dollar-a-day man, doing his bit for the war in Ottawa. But Gabriel only nodded, and I was left feeling that Ottawa could not possibly compare with Washington.

On the wharf we watched the tourist boats chugging towards Percé Rock and the big island. I cheered up a bit when Gabriel offered me a cigarette. I had only smoked one or two in my life, but his Camels looked wonderfully exotic. I had seen advertisements for them on the back covers of American magazines. Gabriel told me that his mother didn't mind his smoking as long as it wasn't done around other adults. It was an arrangement between them and I gathered they had worked out several of these in the conduct of their lives together. We watched girls arm in arm with boyfriends, some of them soldiers, strolling to the end of the wharf to gaze out at the water as people do near lake or sea. Older couples in suits and dresses walked by with their children, speaking French. For me it was like being in a foreign country with the smell of fish and the sea air and the sound of another language in my ears.

When we returned to the hotel, Gabriel directed me to the service elevator near the kitchen. Through an open doorway we could see men and women in white clothes working and hear the clatter of pots and pans. The St. Lawrence Hotel had only three stories, and so there was no elevator for guests, who had to make their own way up the wide carpeted stairs to their rooms. The lift by the kitchen was for the help, a small cage into which I fitted the wheelchair with some difficulty, for there was scarcely enough room for the two of us. Gabriel stabbed the button with one of his canes and we jolted upward, stopping on the third floor at a storage area, a corridor lined with old bedsprings and mattresses, a genuine firetrap when I

think of it now. I pushed him through all this clutter to a door
that opened onto a hall and guest rooms.

It was then mid-afternoon and everyone was downstairs
or outside enjoying the summer day. The world and the war
seemed remote to me there in that hotel hallway as I pushed
Gabriel along to his room. I could hear a radio or a gramophone recording, a woman's voice singing in French. As we
passed an open doorway Gabriel raised an arm, crying, "Halt."
Looking into the room, I saw two girls in their blue and white
uniforms. One was making a bed, holding a pillow against
her chest and fitting it into its case, a cigarette in her mouth.
She was squinting against the smoke. It was the girl I looked
at each day as she went back and forth to work. Although I
hadn't spoken a word to her, I already knew her name. Odette
Huard. The other girl was shorter and plumper and she too
was smoking as she dusted the dresser and mirror. The song
on the radio was wistful and, listening to it, I experienced
one of those unbidden surges of elation that arise from who
knows where. Perhaps it was the sight of Odette. Perhaps it
was the sentimental song on the radio or just the foreignness
of the entire experience. In any case, a moment of incompre-
hensible happiness.

Gabriel was already wagging a finger at the two girls. "Look
here," he said in his English accent, "you're not supposed to
be smoking on the job. I've a good mind to report you to the
management. Just see if I don't. *Comprenez-vous, mademoiselle?*"
The shorter girl was already laughing, but Odette only smiled.
Pointing along the hallway, Gabriel called out, "Ho. Troop forward," and I leaned into the handles of the wheelchair. As I

was to discover in the weeks ahead, this was just another of his fantastical borrowings from the motion pictures. As head of the cavalry troop, he had just received the scout's report; the pass ahead was clear of Indians. Behind us I could hear the two girls speaking French and laughing.

In his room, Gabriel told me that the one making the bed was his girlfriend. "My little cockeyed chambermaid," he called her. "She can speak English," he said. "The other one can't. I talk to Odette every day. Actually we do a lot more than talk." Placing his hands on the wheels of the chair, he pushed himself across the room to a card table upon which lay a partly finished jigsaw puzzle. The picture on the box showed a three-masted schooner making its way through a choppy sea. The project looked huge and difficult, weeks of fitting together pieces of the ship's rigging and the storm-filled sky. Over that summer, Gabriel and his mother and anyone else who entered the room, including myself, would select pieces and spend a few minutes by the card table wondering where to put them. I can't remember but I don't think it was ever completed. As he worked at the puzzle that day, Gabriel talked about a nurse in a hospital in Boston where he had been a patient.

"They had me in for these tests," he said, "and this nurse, boy, was she stacked." He cupped his hands in front of him and grinned at me. "Really stacked. She used to come into my room at night."

I was standing by the window that overlooked the lawn and the flagpole, watching a man and a woman on the tennis court. It was the honeymooners and they were scrambling about the court whacking at the ball. You could see that it was all just a novel experience for them; they couldn't really play the game. I watched them, listening to the *pock, pock* sound of their rackets striking the ball, while Gabriel talked about this nurse and how she used to wake him up at one o'clock in the morning by climbing into his bed.

"I'd wake up and she was unbuttoning her uniform right there and getting into my bed wearing only her bra and panties."

I didn't know whether to believe him or not, but I tried to picture it. In a way, it seemed unlikely. Good-looking or not, he was still a boy in a wheelchair, wasn't he? Could boys like that have sex? Of course they could and can, but I didn't know that, and perhaps out of jealousy or resentment I wished it weren't true. I wanted sex to be off limits to Gabriel Fontaine just as it was to most boys then. Sex was still mysterious and untravelled territory, something most boys at Groveland only talked about. We groped ourselves of course, laughing self-consciously about it, a guilty pleasure. We all lived with a girl in a magazine or in an underwear ad in Eaton's catalogue. Few of us had actually touched a living, naked girl, yet here was this sixteen-year-old American in a wheelchair telling me that a buxom nurse in Boston used to have sex with him at one o'clock in the morning. And it happened a year ago when he was only fifteen. It sounded too good to be true, the ultimate fantasy of every priapic teenage boy in 1944. I wondered about this as I turned from the window to examine the pictures of Hollywood actresses pinned to the walls. Betty Grable in all her leggy gorgeousness, Rita Hayworth coquettishly look-ing back at me over a bare shoulder, an enigmatic Veronica Lake concealing an eye behind that hair. There was also a team picture of the 1943 Boston Red Sox. The place reminded me of some of the rooms at Groveland.

Gabriel must have seen in my face a hint of skepticism about his nurse story.

"You don't believe me, do you, James," he said. "You probably think that because I'm in this chair I can't have sex. Well, you'd be very wrong about that, pal. I can have sex just like anybody else. In fact, I bet I get more than most guys my age. A lot of girls want to see what it's like to have it with someone like me. Others feel sorry for me, I guess, but so what? The point is I get more tail than most guys."

Had I the wit, I could have said that between the curious and the sympathetic, he was doing all right for himself. But of course I only thought about that hours later in bed.

"There are all kinds of women out there, you know," said Gabriel. "That nurse in Boston. She used to like going down on me. It was something, I can tell you."

A nurse *going down on him?* Could it be true? I had heard the phrase at school and had tried to imagine the actual experience, but it all seemed too outlandish. *Going down on him.* I listened, both enthralled and enraged. I imagined tipping over his chair and leaving him sprawled there on the carpet, his arms reaching out for purchase on something, anything, like the stranded crab I had seen that morning on the beach.

Gabriel had wheeled himself across the room and was busy putting one of the thick black discs on the phonograph turntable, settling the needle into the groove. Turning in his chair towards me, he made a fist in front of his mouth, an imaginary microphone. "And now, ladies and gentlemen, the makers of

Old Gold cigarettes are pleased to bring you, from the ball-room of the Waldorf-Astoria Hotel in the heart of Manhattan, the music of Freddy Martin and his orchestra." Raising his hands as if he were a concert pianist, he mimed the opening chords of Martin's theme song, the melody from Tchaikovsky's Concerto No. 1 in B Flat Minor, and began to conduct the music, smiling desperately throughout this performance. His timing was impeccable. He must have practised this stunt for hours, and I had to laugh at his antics. All right, he was an insufferable American braggart but an entertaining one all the same.

That afternoon, we listened to dance-band music. Tommy Dorsey, Benny Goodman, Artie Shaw. There was also an album from the musical *Oklahoma!* which his mother had taken him to see in New York. Apparently they went often to the magical city to see dramas and musical comedies, or to Yankee Stadium when the Red Sox were in town. Did I like baseball? Did we have dances at our school or at a nearby girls' school as they did at his? Weren't most rich girls fatheaded and boring? He preferred nurses and maids. They were more down-to-earth and knew about life. In my year at Groveland, I had grown accustomed to the bragging of boarding school boys. But never had I met anyone so flamboyantly full of himself as Gabriel Fontaine. And I must have been the perfect audience for him, a provincial who really hadn't been anywhere. I would soon grow used to Gabriel's ways, however; I could feel myself growing used to them that afternoon, felt my anger and jealousy abating, for there was an openness to him, an amiability that was hard to resist, even though, as I discovered in time, it masked a terrible cruelty. I suppose to some, perhaps to women, it would have been called charm. I know that I stayed far too long in his hotel room that Saturday afternoon. Beyond the window the shadows lengthened across the lawn and the empty tennis court and still we sat listening to music and smoking our Camels. I say smoking, but in my case, I was faking it; I had never really learned how to inhale. Still it felt wonderfully grown up to be sitting there with a cigarette in my hand.

We exchanged stories about our schools, though I could tell Gabriel wasn't much interested in my experiences. He never was. He would listen and nod, but he was always anxious to get back to his own narrative, which I had to admit was more interesting than mine. Polio had struck him five years earlier at summer camp. Several boys were afflicted. The doctors told him he would never walk again, but he refused to believe it and so on. A familiar tale of heroism in the face of the odds and the naysayers. Every time I thought of leaving, he pressed another Coke or cigarette on me, and in spite of my not inhaling, I was beginning to feel a little queasy. But I knew that my uncle would probably be furious and that helped. Gabriel wanted to know if Uncle Chester was queer. He thought he must be, given his mannerisms. He told me there were men like him at his school. I said I didn't really know or care about that, and I could see that he found my casual attitude about it a bit peculiar. Perhaps he thought that afternoon I too was a homosexual.

About five o'clock his mother knocked on the door and came in. I thought she would be irritated by the smoky, stinky air—we'd both been farting all afternoon and laughing about it, as boys do—but Mrs. Fontaine took no notice. There she was with her radiant smile, exclaiming, "So here is where all the handsome young men in town are."

"Hello, Mother dear," said Gabriel.

The way he said it sounded not quite right to me. Was he mocking her, I wondered? But she said only, "We've been looking all over for you two. We didn't imagine you'd be up here on such a beautiful day. James, your uncle is beside himself. I fear you've put poor Chester off his schedule. He's worrying about your landlady and the dinner hour."

I was glad she was there. I enjoyed looking at Mrs. Fontaine almost as much as I enjoyed looking at Odette Huard. I was learning that there were all sorts of female beauty in the world. The dance band music on the phonograph now had a Latin flavour, a rumba or a samba, and Mrs. F was taken by its infectious rhythm. Removing the scarf from around her throat, she held it above her head while she swayed to the music. Perhaps she was a little drunk. I thought I'd smelled liquor on her when she came into the room. It didn't matter. I was a moth in her flame, drawn to the sight of this middle-aged woman, a boy's mother, dancing for us, mesmerized by her trim backside and the red toenails in her sandals as she took intricate little steps in perfect time to the music. From his wheelchair Gabriel was shouting, "*Olé.*"

That Friday evening I was again walking down Park Lane but this time on my way to The Dorchester for dinner with Gabriel Fontaine. It was dusk and taxi drivers had turned on their lights. People were out with dogs or hurrying past to an early supper before the theatre. I was moved by the thought of dinner with Gabriel. What had he done with all those years since we had last seen each other?

I was feeling a mild flutter of excitement, and I was touched also by the evening itself, its autumnal air. I have always been affected by weather in all its guises. My mother was the same. She was often to be seen on the veranda of our house on Crescent Road, peering up through the tree branches at the sky, alert for a change in the wind. As a child, I would sometimes hear her getting up before daybreak in winter, a storm raging beyond the windows. I used to sit unseen at the top of the stairs, and watch her putting on galoshes and coat, her old brown tam. How I hated that tam! I thought it made her look a bit crazy. She would open the front door to all that howling, and after she closed it behind her, I felt as if she were walking out of my life and might never return. Yet I know now why she did such things. She wanted to experience the fury of it all, and perhaps too she found beauty in it. On chilly mornings in April, she would sit on a bench at the bottom of the garden wrapped in her winter coat and tam, waiting for the birds to awaken and sing. I often arose and, kneeling by the window, watched her figure emerging from the darkness. So even there, in the centre of London, I still felt the natural world around me; perhaps it was the great park across the street, the look of the plane trees in the darkening sky. In any case, I was struck by how happy I might have been, had I not a daughter who was dying, for of course I was also thinking of Susan.

Thinking of her walking through the same evening seventy miles to the northwest in Oxfordshire. I pictured her crossing the playing fields, watching the girls on their way to the library or returning to their Houses after supper. I knew that Susan would also be moved by the simple beauty of the evening. She would be taking it in, and now in the middle of her forty-sixth year perhaps wondering if it wasn't too much to ask that she be granted other evenings like this in the years ahead. But such requests are not granted to some, and now she was a member of that "some." What must first strike you in such circumstances is the terrible unfairness of it all. But unfairness in what sense? The concept of fairness or unfairness in life implies order and meaning, some judicial hand determining human destinies. In other words, the belief in a deity. Woolford Abbey was ostensibly a Christian school, though from the look of the student body, at least a third of them must have been Muslim or Hindu or something else. Still it was, at least in name, a community of believers. The chapel service was Anglican and as headmistress, Susan would have had to profess at least some articles of faith. Or would she have? Would such questions be asked nowadays by a hiring committee? I am well out of things and do not know the answers to such questions. It was strange but the subject had never arisen during my stay with her. That in itself could be telling, though at the very least I guessed that Susan was probably agnostic. No one to pray to then or shake a fist at. And even had I been asked, I could have offered no comfort.

A former friend, Catherine Parmeter, and I used to discuss such matters, and though we had both defined our positions, we still enjoyed talking about religion. Catherine belongs to an Anglo-Catholic congregation in Toronto, and now and then I would go along to her church. I enjoyed listening to the language of the prayer book and the choir's singing of the anthems. All of it was pleasing in an aesthetic way, but for me there was nothing more than that. It was much like going to a recital or a concert. I missed Catherine. She would have been the perfect person to talk to after Susan's call, but she was in New Zealand on her sabbatical, and no doubt sleeping with a man I knew would eventually disappoint her.

Catherine is thirteen years younger than I am and still very much a player in the sexual comedy. The man had come to Toronto as a visiting professor the year before. His field was Catholic thought and literature from Newman to Greene. Something like that. It's odd how Catholicism seems to inspire carnality in educated or talented people. Greene, I believe, was an avid fornicator and always in the confession box about it. Early on, I sensed that something was happening between Catherine and this fellow. Whenever I prepared a meal for her or we went to the theatre, his name would emerge. "A fascinating man," she called him on more than one occasion. I'm sure they began their affair that autumn. I met him just once, at a dinner party among old colleagues from the English department. He was the guest of honour, a florid, burly character in his fifties. Handsome enough in a dissolute way. Probably a boozer. I envisioned him collapsing in the midst of a heavy meal. Or after sex. No matter, Catherine was taken with the brute, and on a holiday in Bermuda between Christmas and New Year's (the day after Susan left for England in fact), Catherine told me that her sabbatical had been approved and she would be going to Auckland that summer. To which I said something prissily stupid like "Very well" or "If you must." I was jealous and angry, though Catherine didn't owe me anything, least of all lifelong companionship. Still, I miss her. So I felt very much alone walking down Park Lane that Friday evening. Alone with these appalling conclusions: Susan could easily leave the world before me and I would never see her again. Never watch another movie with her or discuss another book. *Never, never, never, never, never.* The old king's lamentation, but I know of none better. Yet how quickly our thoughts and feelings, however sombre, are temporarily shunted onto a siding by a change in circumstances or setting; at once our minds must cope with new experience.

In the hotel lobby I was instantly among people being professionally cosseted, all services and comforts attended to with a friendly look and not a manufactured one either. Not the rictus of the coffee counter or doughnut shop, the "have a nice day" smile. No, indeed. In a hotel like The Dorchester, you are offered a more natural arrangement of the features, a smile that conveys the impression that you will be well looked after under this roof. My twenty-year-old raincoat, for instance, was taken without a trace of condescension by an attractive young woman. Another led me past the tables with their silverware and folded napery. The dining room wasn't yet busy, a foursome of Japanese, an elderly couple at a corner table, an older man and a young woman raising their glasses in a toast. A romantic encounter? A salute to erotic novelty ahead? I must have been thinking of Catherine and her Kiwi.

Gabriel was alone at his table, the wheelchair against a wall so that I could see only a small pale figure behind the flowers. He was wearing a dark suit with a white shirt and a beautiful maroon tie. As I approached, I wondered about all the bother of dressing, the many years of untangling shirt sleeves and trouser legs, the help with underclothes, one's parts exposed to whomever was assisting. Oddly enough, I remembered having something like the same thoughts when I first stood behind his wheelchair over sixty years before. Yet despite the shrunkenness, the obvious fragility, Gabriel looked distinguished in a gloomy sort of way. I think it was the hair, now long and silvery, well brushed. I pictured Adam standing over Gabriel, brushing all that hair while the old man closed his eyes in contentment. It was quite an impressive mane, and along with the scowl, made him look like some old, cranky orchestral figure, a Herbert von Karajan type. As always in his company, I felt hopelessly plain.

"James," he said, looking up at me, "good of you to come on such short notice. What a treat this is for me! Seeing you after all these years. I've been thinking about you all afternoon."

He had shaved, or very likely had been shaven, for I could now see the tremor in his hands. A touch of Parkinson's? I could also smell the lotion. A common habit of the elderly, to douse ourselves with scent in the hope of concealing the smells of age and sickness.

A waiter came by and asked about drinks. Gabriel implored me to have something. "It will do me good to watch you," he said. "I can't drink any more."

So I treated myself to a twelve-year-old single malt that I hadn't enjoyed for a long time. Gabriel said I should also think about some wine with dinner.

"They have an excellent cellar, James. If you like good wine, you couldn't ask for a better place to be." He told me that his body could no longer metabolize alcohol. It was failing him, he said. "The whole damn thing is shutting down and I'm just as glad. It's time. To hell with it."

In saying this he sounded almost buoyant, and then for a few moments neither of us said anything. We seemed suddenly awkward in each other's company. I sat there remembering the good-looking boy in Percé, Quebec, in 1944, watching his long white hand reach for the water glass and raise it trem-blingly to his lips. At such times we are often compelled to observe simple acts, hoping they will be accomplished with-out the embarrassment of something spilled down a shirt front. When finally he'd had his sip and successfully returned the glass to the table, I asked what had brought him to England. He laughed unpleasantly as if I'd posed a foolish question.

"I'm just passing through," he said. "I'm on my way to Zurich, Switzerland. Leaving Sunday morning."

How well I could recall the sound of that jeering laughter, and I felt almost immediately the onset of an old anger. Couldn't help myself. I hadn't been there five minutes and already I was growing cross with him. Poor old bugger.

He was now attacking a hard roll, the fingers digging and tearing away at the crust, absorbed as old people can be when they are wrestling with tasks that once were child's play. We both watched in silence while he worked at this. I was thinking that he had to be very rich. The cut of his clothes. Staying at The Dorchester. A man to look after him. It took a great deal of money to move around the world like that. But when I thought of it, wasn't Zurich one of the banking and financial centres of Europe? Was Gabriel going there to check on his numbered accounts, his store of bullion hoarded against possible market collapse?

The waiter brought my drink while Gabriel broke through the roll's defences and began to butter a fragment. "You should try the steak, James. Adam says it's the best he's ever tasted."

But over the years I have gradually lost my taste for red meat. I still eat my daughter-in-law's roast beef dinners, which are essentially the same meals I was served each Sunday as a child on Crescent Road. I still eat them because not to do so would require a lengthy explanation that I never feel like going into with Brenda. She's an old-fashioned girl who is uncomfortable with change. I've wondered from time to time whether my son, David, moved out because he just grew tired of all those Sunday roast beef dinners. So I chose the salmon with a glass of Chablis, while Gabriel muttered "The usual" to the waiter.

"I've been thinking about you all afternoon, James," he said. "I've been remembering that summer in Quebec. You were a good friend to me then. You pushed me all over that little town."

How we old survivors tend to edit our memories! Had he forgotten how angry I was with him on that last day?

"Remember the French girl, Yvette?" he asked. "She was a pretty little thing. We had a lot of fun together."

"Her name was Odette, Gabriel," I said.

He frowned. "Odette? That's funny. I remember her as Yvette."

"No, no," I said. "Her name was Odette. Odette Huard. She lived next door to the house I was staying in with my uncle. Odette Huard. That was her name and maybe still is for all I know. She could still be alive. She'd be about your age. A year younger, as I recall. She was fifteen that summer. You thought she was sixteen, but she wasn't. She was only fifteen."

This outburst surprised both of us, and he looked at me with the air of a man who was not used to being contradicted and was now wondering how to proceed. But then he also looked suddenly, massively tired. He seemed to droop in his wheelchair, shrugging and offering only a weak smile. I heard the faintest intonation of old Humphrey Bogart as he said, "Well, if you say so, pal, but I remember her as Yvette."

The whisky had emboldened me, and I said to myself that it

was not going to be like the old days. Ill and miserable though he was, I was going to stand my ground with Gabriel Fontaine. After a moment he leaned forward.

"Are you over here on business, James, or a holiday?"

"I'm here to see my daughter," I said. "She's not well. Not well at all."

Gabriel nodded, but typically didn't ask for details, and that too was irritating. Not even the simplest inquiry or expression of sympathy. *What's the problem? How is she? That's too bad. I'm sorry to hear it.* There before me was the same old Gabriel, self-absorbed and fundamentally indifferent to what was going on in another life.

"How long are you staying in England?" he asked.

"I'm returning to Canada on Sunday," I said. "Why do you ask?"

"I assume you're retired from whatever you did."

"Professor of Victorian literature, yes." The tone of my voice, the brisk responses to his questions, none of it raised an eyebrow in curiosity or perturbation.

"So you have no definite plans, then? You don't necessarily have to go back to Canada on Sunday?"

"In the broadest sense, no, though of course there are people who will be expecting me then."

"A mere matter of getting in touch with them," he said, "a phone call, or an e-mail if you do that sort of thing. A simple change in plans." All this with a faint smile.

"I suppose so, yes," I said, "but what on earth are you getting at?"

"Would you do me a great favour, James?"

"That depends on what it is," I said. "Look, Gabriel, we haven't seen each other in sixty years and, to tell you the truth, earlier this afternoon when I first saw you, or rather heard you, I very nearly passed by, thinking he won't remember me so why bother. So the connection between us, you must admit, is at best fairly tenuous. And I've just had a difficult few days with my daughter who is gravely ill. So when you ask me for a favour, I really need to know what you would like me to do before I say yes or no." With that little peroration, I finished my drink.

"I'm sorry, James," he said. "I should have asked about your daughter."

I waited and then said, "Do you have children, Gabriel?"

"No," he said, reaching again for the water glass. "No children. Three wives over a lifetime, but no children. Never really wanted them."

I should have asked about your daughter. But he didn't, did he. And watching another shaky trip of the glass to his lips, I was hoping he'd spill most of it on his hundred-dollar tie. Then he asked me to go to Zurich with him.

"All expenses looked after. First class. A day or two there and we'll fly you back to Canada. Again first class. You'll be home by Tuesday or Wednesday. Or you can stay as long as you like. Have a bit of a holiday."

I was wishing I had a little more Scotch in my glass. "Why would you want me to go to Switzerland with you, Gabriel?"

"I need a friend along," he said. "Even a friend from over half a century ago. In fact, it occurred to me this afternoon when we were talking outside the hotel that you might be the best kind of friend to have along. We could talk a bit about that summer together. It's all coming back to me since I laid eyes on you, James."

As he chewed a little on a piece of his roll, the irony of his situation didn't escape me; wealthy as he appeared to be, he seemed reduced to a diet of bread and water.

"Adam's a good fellow in his own way," he said. "He looks after me. Feeds me my cereal in the morning if I'm having a weak spell. Lines up my daily dose of pills. Wipes my backside after the morning shit. If and when I can shit. Tucks me in at night. But he's paid to do all that. The man's a trained nurse. It's what he does for a living. What I'd like is a friend along with me—and then when you showed up like that this afternoon, why it seemed . . . I can't think of the goddamn word."

"Fortuitous?" I suggested.

"*Fortuitous.* Exactly. That's the word."

"Why are you going to Zurich?" I asked.

"I'm going there to die, James," he said. "Don't worry, it's all legal. They're very enlightened about these things, the Europeans. They'll put you out of your misery swiftly and painlessly. I've been in touch with an organization there and in fact Adam and I flew to Zurich a few weeks ago. Labour Day weekend. You have to have an interview with them so they can check your case, medical history and so on. You have to be on the way out before they'll deal with you. Nice people. Very professional. It's all set for Monday morning at ten o'clock."

"You're going to commit suicide, then?"

Gabriel had settled back in his chair, looking tired but pleased with himself.

"In a manner of speaking, yes. But it will all be done professionally in the presence of a doctor. I'm not going to wheel this goddamn chair off a mountain or blow my brains out. It's going to be done right. Good God, man, surely you can tell looking at me that I've got only a few months left and every day is a fucking torment. I've got pancreatic cancer. I can't wait to get it over with."

More cancer, then. But why be surprised? I thought. It was the plague of an aging society. Living longer to suffer more. And Gabriel was getting up there. So was I, for that matter. You have to die of something sooner or later. Now Susan, on the other hand . . . But I couldn't bear to go down that road just then.

The waiter brought our dinners, my plate of salmon and vegetables and Gabriel's dish of what looked like rice pudding but was in fact a risotto. I was thinking about his proposition. Accompany him to Switzerland where he intended to have himself put to death. I could remember reading a newspaper article about euthanasia in Switzerland. Apparently some members of their parliament had raised a fuss about admitting foreigners whose sole purpose in visiting the country was to arrange their own exits. According to these politicians, Switzerland was projecting the wrong image to the world with these so-called death tourists. At the time, I wondered if those indignant parliamentarians were happier with the country's image as a place where American gangsters and African dictators could stow their billions. Moral confusion everywhere. What would Alfred T have made of it all?

I told Gabriel I was sorry to hear about his poor health, but he only waved a languid hand.

"Don't be. I'm ready to go. Looking forward to it." He leaned over his bowl of rice and I could see that this movement caused him some pain.

"This is the happiest I've been in months," he said, wincing as he settled back again. "It would be nice, though," he said, "to have someone like you along. Someone who knows me. Or at least knows a bit of me. Someone who isn't just paid to be there."

All this with the old boyish smile. He might have been asking me to wheel him down to the wharf. Take him for a "spin" so we could see if there were any pretty girls visiting.

"What did your doctors think of your decision?" I asked.

Gabriel shrugged. "What do I care what they think? Those bastards have to keep you alive no matter how fucked up you are. That's their job. This has to do with me, not them."

The people at the next table had obviously overheard him and were casting glances our way. I don't know why I should have, but I found it amusing—Gabriel's spunky attitude about the medical profession, which is so often unquestioningly revered. The place was filling up.

"Gabriel," I said, "I wouldn't mind another glass of this truly splendid wine."

This delighted him. "And you shall have it, sir, and immediately." He was already waving at a waiter.

"How do they go about this?" I asked.

"In Zurich, you mean?"

"Yes."

"They explained it all clearly when we were there last month. We will go to a house somewhere in the city on Monday morning, and a doctor and a nurse will be there. They'll provide a sedative and then, after a few minutes, my glass of hemlock. I have to take it myself. I soon fall asleep and then I expire. They then arrange to have me cremated and my ashes sent back to the States, where they'll be interred in the family plot."

It all sounded so rational. So sensible. Because when you think about it, how do most of us die? Often gasping for breath, clutching bedclothes in a sweaty terror. Or wincing and waiting for the nurse and the next shot of painkiller, as I guessed Gabriel was doing at that very moment. How many of us are lucky enough to die in our sleep, borne unaware into oblivion?

"I'm on my way out," he said. "As far as I'm concerned, going to Zurich beats lying in bed for the next three months being looked after by strangers. Wasting away. That's what you do, you know. You waste away. Cancer literally eats you from the inside out. Think about it, James."

I *was* thinking about it. Had been thinking about it all week, as he would have known had he bothered to ask about my daughter. Yet despite old reawakened irritations, I felt sorry for him. Another suffering mortal. We're all in the same boat. He wanted to talk then about the next day—his last in London—when he and Adam were going in a hired car to have a final look at the old city. He intended, insofar as his memory would permit, to replicate his first visit. A Sunday afternoon in the summer of 1938. He was ten years old. That day he and his parents were in an enormous black car with a chauffeur at the wheel. They came upon a demonstration. Near St. Paul's Cathedral. Men in black shirts were marching with banners and were being taunted by people lining the street. Others shouted their support. There were fist fights and a great many policemen. Bobbies they were called and they wore those tall helmets, and one of them waved the big car down a side street away from the turmoil. Gabriel's father approved of the demonstrators. They were against the Communists and deserved to be applauded. His mother agreed. It was a day Gabriel said he would never forget. But his reminiscence seemed to wear him down and now he looked unwell. When the waiter brought me another glass of wine, Gabriel told him that he wanted someone to call his room. He'd hardly touched his risotto.

Around us was the laughter and conversation of people enjoying their Friday night dinners with no thought, I'm sure, for their mortal state. And why should they have had? But I thought of Susan and our meal a few nights earlier in the little restaurant in Woolford. Was Gabriel also looking at others with the envy of the doomed? But really he seemed too ill to be bothered.

I don't know whether I had thought it all through. I don't expect I had, but nevertheless I said I'd go with him to Zurich. At once he reached across the table and grasped my hand in both of his.

"Thank you for that, James," he said, and then we both sat there in silence, embarrassed by the emotion in the air.

I sipped my wine and Gabriel cast a glaring eye over the restaurant while we waited for Adam, who arrived in a few minutes looking concerned but perfectly dressed in a smart grey suit. I pictured him sitting in that hotel room all evening in that suit with nowhere to go except down to the dining room to fetch his master.

"Get me out of here," said Gabriel.

"Of course, sir."

Gabriel was pointing a finger at me. "Mr. Hillyer is coming with us on Sunday, Adam. I want you to make the necessary arrangements."

"Yes, sir," said Adam, who had already stationed himself behind the old man, ready to wheel him out. But then Gabriel gave him the old wait-a-minute palm-upward that I remembered so well.

"James," said Gabriel. "Why don't you go to the bar after your dinner and have a glass of brandy? Enjoy a nightcap while Adam tucks me in. Then he can join you for a few minutes. He'll have to know your flight information so he can arrange things. And you can get to know each other. After all, we're going to be travelling companions. How does that sound?"

"Fine, Gabriel," I said, "I'm not in any hurry."

"Good. And take a taxi back to your hotel. You never can tell who's roaming the streets nowadays. We don't want anything to happen to you—do we, Adam?"

"No indeed, sir."

"I'll see you Sunday morning, James," he said, pointing forward with a long bony finger. "Let's go."

In the bar I ordered a Calvados, a drink Catherine Parmeter and I used to occasionally enjoy together at the end of a meal. I hadn't been on a bar stool in years, and sitting there I felt as if I were about to set forth on an adventure with only a vague idea of how it might work out. Such moments of course can be exhilarating, and are all too rare as we grow older. I was there nursing my Calvados for perhaps twenty minutes before Adam Trench arrived. He gave me his surname later in our conversation. Adam didn't drink alcohol and ordered a club soda. We sat there side by side looking perhaps like an old man with his young paramour. I asked him how he came by his job, and he told me he'd been working as a nurse in a Boston hospital and had read an advertisement a year ago for a personal assistant with a medical background. The compensation was attractive and there were many applicants, but, as Adam told me, success in his line of work depends to a large extent on the chemistry between the patient and the person assisting him. As it turned out, he and Mr. Fontaine hit it off from the start.

I pointed out that it must be hard working for someone like Gabriel who was so demanding. "You must be a saint," I said.

"Not so, Dr. Hillyer," he said. "I'm no saint."

"Well, you seem like one to me," I said, "and please, if it bothers you to call an old guy like me by his first name, then Mr. Hillyer will do nicely. But no Dr. Hillyer, please. Such designations are taken seriously only inside the Academy and even there only by the hidebound or delusional."

Adam agreed that Mr. Fontaine could be difficult, but it had to be kept in mind that he was very ill and didn't mean half of what he said. "My job is to see to his comfort and not complain about his manner."

What a decent fellow he was, this young man from Indianapolis with his blond good looks and calm reserve! I managed to get him talking about himself, though he was guarded and selective about details. His father had been a doctor in the air force, and as a young family they had moved around from base to base both in America and Europe. When he became a teenager, he was enrolled in a military academy, where he spent the next several years. It was an unhappy period, for he was temperamentally ill-suited to the rigorously macho atmosphere of such places. He wanted to become a doctor like his father, but his grades weren't strong enough, and he had to settle for nursing, which apparently didn't please Dr. Trench. Adam left the Midwest for Boston, and a few years later was fortunate to meet "the love of his life," who was ten years older, an art dealer with his own gallery. Adam seemed proud of him. All this further estranged him from his family, but he was happy now, living in a city of which he had become fond, and with someone who loved and understood him. He and Donald were Baha'is. I had never met anyone from the Baha'i community before and I was curious. Adam, however, was not particularly forthcoming; he said only that they did not proselytize but believed in tolerance and respect for the faiths of others. I asked him how he felt about Gabriel's decision to end his life in Zurich.

"It's his choice, Mr. Hillyer. It's not for us to judge, is it. We must respect a person's decisions." He was looking straight ahead and seemed uneasy discussing such matters.

I said, "Well, Gabriel is fortunate to have you looking after him as he nears the end of his life."

But Adam wasn't interested in compliments, and turning to me, he smiled. "Mr. Fontaine told me about your summer together in Quebec many years ago. He said you were a good friend to him and you had some wonderful times together."

"Partly true," I said.

"It's very good of you to come along with us, sir. It means a great deal to Mr. Fontaine."

I wanted to know about Gabriel's evident wealth. What had he worked at all his life? Had he worked at all? Adam told me that of course he'd only known Gabriel for a year, but he gathered that Mr. Fontaine had been a partner in a large brokerage firm. And there'd been family money as well. I could see, however, that Adam was becoming a little anxious at being away too long from his patient. He wanted to get down to business, and asked me where I was staying so that he could phone about details for Sunday morning. What airline was I currently using and when did I want to return to Canada?

"I suppose it might as well be Tuesday, Adam," I said.

"I'll see to it."

He was writing it all down in a little notebook, and watching him, I felt the mild trepidation we sometimes experience when we see another person doing just that—writing down things that will arrange our lives in a slightly different way. But it was too late to change my mind.

As he wrote, Adam said, "Tomorrow Mr. Fontaine is going to have a final look around London. He told me that when he was ten years old his mother and father took him on a tour of the city. They were on a holiday, just the three of them in a big black car with a driver. It was the summer of 1938. He told me he can remember everything about that Sunday. There was a political demonstration in the streets. Men in black shirts, marching. I found it interesting listening to him. It was the summer before he got polio. The last summer he would walk and run. He wants to make that tour again tomorrow. Along the Strand and over by St. Paul's Cathedral."

As I listened to what I already knew, I marvelled at Adam, who actually sounded as if he were looking forward to all this, to indulging an old man's nostalgia, to a Saturday afternoon that most people would find wearisome beyond words. Or was he merely playing the role of the faithful and willing servant? It was hard to know. He then said that he should be getting back up to the suite and would be in touch. He also told me to take a taxi to my hotel. Mr. Fontaine had insisted and everything had been arranged with the doorman. I had only to ask.

very day I watched Odette Huard from my little screened window in Mrs. Moore's attic. I watched her as she left in the morning and as she returned from Percé in the late afternoon. Watched her as she oversaw the antics of her brothers and sisters in the long evenings of early summer. The Huards kept to themselves and appeared to have no other playmates but each other, and so there was often bickering and quarrels, and I knelt there listening to the laughter and the tears as moods shifted and voices called to each other in French. Sometimes Odette would join in their games, throwing a ball or chasing a sister or brother around the house. Mostly, however, she would sit on the gallery steps watching them. Now and then her mother, a pale thin woman, would come out and sit next to her oldest child on the steps. Where, I wondered, was Mr. Huard? What did they live on? They were poor. That was easy to see, but they still had to eat and buy clothes and wood for the stove. At my window I watched Odette examining her bare feet or scratching her behind. I was as attentive to this slim, dark-haired girl across the field as any besotted peeping Tom. She was the object of the virtually uncontrollable lust that blossoms in a boy at the beginning of his sexual life when he discovers the ease with which he can be transported into bliss. When my knees got tired, I would pull my chair over to the window, but that made me stoop and soon I was on my knees again with a sore neck.

Monday was Odette's day off, and to get away from the commotion of the yard, she would set out by herself for a few hours in the morning. A week had passed since my Saturday afternoon with Gabriel and I hadn't been back to the St. Lawrence Hotel. My uncle was cross with me. In snubbing the Fontaines' hospitality, he said, I was being rude and obstinate, an embarrassment to him personally. This was true and I was happy enough to see him upset, but I had no intention of changing my mind. As far as I was concerned, the rich American kid could find someone else to push his wheelchair around. I told Uncle Chester that I was devoting the rest of the summer to the study of trigonometry, which only made him smirk. I was, however, reading *Great Expectations* and memorizing some of Tennyson's poems. "The splendour falls on castle walls / And snowy summits old in story." All that, I decided, along with spying on Odette Huard, would constitute my summer pastimes.

On that Monday morning I watched Odette walking down the lane wearing a housedress and a cardigan sweater and those awful Mary Jane shoes with ankle socks that girls wore then. Near the gate she stopped to scold one of the younger children who was following her, pointing back to the house until the child obeyed. That too I found alluring, that blend of maternal concern and sexuality. She seemed years older than she looked, but I guessed she was no more than sixteen. The sight of her that summer morning left me turbulent with desire. Following her, I watched with disappointment as she turned in to the general store. On an errand for her mother, then. I had hoped to follow her past the village to a path along the cliff, where I imagined her stopping to gaze out to sea like some girl on the cover of a romance novel, a girl wondering what lay ahead and where was the boy who would rescue her from her life as a chambermaid and surrogate mother, a boy whose heart was also filled with longing and poetry.

Instead I took the path along the cliff by myself and then followed another down to a little cove where I liked to sit on the rocks. I had discovered the cove the day after I arrived in the village—a secluded haven where I thought I was safe from prying eyes. There beneath the cliff I was free to indulge my dream of undressing Odette Huard. And so I did, in a few frantic moments, the seed of Onan spilling once again on the ground. But as I leaned panting against the rock face, I heard something above me, a rustling among the weeds and wildflowers. Unloosed pebbles were falling through the grass. I buttoned myself hastily, but I was mortified, because moments later I glanced up and saw Odette Huard making her way along the path towards me.

Had she seen me, then? Would she be smiling at the thought of telling the other maid at the St. Lawrence Hotel and perhaps even Gabriel Fontaine? I felt like running along the shore as fast as my legs would take me. Running back to my attic room, from which I would not emerge until the end of the summer. Mrs. Moore could leave my meals by the door. But all I did was stand there watching Odette come down the path. She wasn't smiling; she was frowning in concentration, for it was steep and precarious. As she drew nearer, I could see that she had a cast in one eye, a slight turning to the right. That was what Gabriel must have been thinking about when he called her his cockeyed little chambermaid.

She didn't appear surprised to see me there. "You're staying in the Moores' house, aren't you?" she said.

"Yes."

"I saw you last week at the hotel. You were with the crippled American boy."

"Yes, I was."

She had taken off the cardigan and put one hand on the cliff face. "It's going to be hot today," she said as she took off her shoes and socks.

I could see the swell of her breasts and the hair under her arms as she stood first on one leg and then on the other. Carrying the shoes and socks she jumped lightly between the rocks to the little sandy beach, where for a few moments she stood in the water. Then she came back and sat down on the sand.

Looking back at me she called, "He's very funny that friend of yours."

"He's not a friend of mine," I said, walking towards her.

She must have caught something in my voice, for she smiled. "Why don't you sit down and have a conversation with me? We're neighbours, aren't we?"

"I suppose we are, yes."

It is not easy for a girl to sit on the sand in a dress with a boy beside her. Either she draws her knees towards her and hugs them with both arms for modesty's sake, or else she stretches them out. Odette stretched out her legs, leaning back on her elbows and staring at the water. I couldn't take my eyes off the sand that clung to her feet. She was looking at me.

"Do you like it here in the village? It can't be much fun. You don't speak French, do you?"

"No," I said.

She shrugged. "It doesn't matter. It's mostly English around here. I'm from Montreal. We're just staying here while my father makes some money for us." She was still looking at me. "What's your name?"

"James," I said.

"Mine is Odette."

"Yes, I know."

"Why is your face so red? It's like a big tomato. Your ears are red too." I looked away. "Maybe you don't talk much to girls," she said. "Is that it?"

"Something like that maybe."

"Well, don't worry, I won't bite."

"I'm not worried."

It was a still morning and a haze lay across the water. Gulls wheeled and squawked. Now and then, over the wash of the sea, we could hear a car passing on the road above the cliffs.

"Do you like it here?" Odette asked.

"Yes," I lied. "It's very beautiful."

"I thought you might say that," she said. "Everybody who comes here says that. And it's true, I guess. But do you really *like* it here? You don't do anything but stay in that house and look out at me."

Shocked? Yes, of course, though flustered would better describe it. All along, then, she had known I was watching her, my hapless moonlike face at the window, as tormented and crazy in my own way as the man with all that electricity inside him on the street next to ours in Toronto.

"Yes," Odette said, "I've seen you looking out at me through your little window." Then she did a wonderful thing. A miraculous thing to me. She sat up and, as if we were already old friends, she gave me a quick hug. "Oh, don't take it all so seriously," she whispered. "I'm just teasing you. I don't care really. It's nice to be looked at." Her warm breath in my ear. I had never been that close to a girl. Again she leaned back on her elbows. "I knew your name before today. Gabriel told me."

"Did you tell him that all I do is look out the window at you?"

She laughed. "No. Why would I do that?" I shrugged, and she said, "He wonders why you haven't come back to see him. He mentioned it one day. He likes you. He doesn't get much company."

I was imagining the both of them talking about me.

"That Gabriel," she said, "he's always making fun of Pauline and me, but he doesn't really mean it. It's just his way. He's very generous. He gives us things."

"Like what?" I asked.

She was sitting up now, hugging her knees and looking out at the water. "Cigarettes. Coca-Cola. He gave me a book last week. I said I liked reading, so he gave me this book." She laughed. "It's got some dirty parts in it. He underlined them." I was looking at the turning in her hazel eye. I liked it. "Gabriel's funny," she said. "He plays his dance music when Pauline and me are cleaning his room. He sits there conducting the band, and I always find that . . ." She stopped. "There's a word in English meaning 'very funny.' It starts with the letter *haitch*."

"*Haitch?*"

"Yes. *Haitch* like in *hill* or *hat*."

"Hilarious?"

"Yes. Hilarious, that's it." She said it slowly, pronouncing all four syllables. It's hilarious when he does that." I didn't say anything and then she said, "But he's brave too. Gabriel will never dance to that music, and that's very sad when you think about it."

"I guess so," I said. "I don't know him very well. I just met him that once. That Saturday you saw us together. My uncle wanted me to meet him. It was all his idea."

She was looking sideways at me, resting her head on her knees. "You don't like Gabriel?"

"He's all right."

Odette then took her sweater and made a little pillow behind her. She lay down and, using a hand to shield her eyes from the sun, looked up at me again. It was funny but it all seemed so natural to be there with her. We'd really only known each other for ten minutes, but she had that way about her, a forthright nature that allowed her to enter your life almost immediately. With only a handful of scattered facts to go on, she led the way, so that in no time at all you felt free to comment or argue with her.

"Your uncle writes books, doesn't he?" she asked.

"Yes," I said. "Books for children. They're not very good. Silly really."

She was staring up at the sky with the little roof of her hand across her eyes.

"Well," she said, "it's something to write books. Any kind of books. I would like to write a book someday. You should be proud of your uncle."

Proud of Uncle Chester? The thought had never crossed my mind.

I may have shrugged again, or she saw something in my face, for she said, "Why are you such a sorehead, anyway? You don't like Gabriel. You think your uncle writes silly books. And all you do in this beautiful place is stay up in that room and peek at me when I'm hanging out the family bloomers." Sitting up again she gave me a little push, which caught me off balance. I nearly toppled. "I think you are just not used to girls," she said. "How old are you anyway?"

"Sixteen," I said.

"Ha. I'll bet not. You don't sound like sixteen to me." She lay down again. "More like fifteen, I'd say. Maybe even fourteen . . ."

"Gabriel told you how old I am."

She smiled. "Maybe."

"So why ask if you already know? Just to make fun of me?"

"Maybe."

"Anyway, how does sixteen sound? Like Gabriel, I suppose."

Odette had closed her eyes, and now I could look at her as she lay there.

"Gabriel," she murmured, "sometimes sounds more like twenty-one." She lay as though sleeping with an arm across her forehead and this lifted a breast inside that flimsy house-dress. She spoke as if in sleep. "Gabriel told me you were only fourteen. So you see I have already caught you out in a lie. The first time we talk and you lie to me." Then abruptly she sat up. She knew that I had been staring down at her. I was angry.

"You're French," I said. "Where did you learn to speak English?"

"In Montreal," she said. "I grew up in Montreal. I'm only here for a while. My father lives in Montreal. He works in a fac-tory where they make gun shells and bombs. He earns good money after being out of work for a long time. This is only our first year here. My father moved us here last October because it's cheap. A cousin of ours owns the house. He works at the same place as my father, but he doesn't have as many kids, so he moved his family up there. I have seven brothers and sis-ters. Try to find a house in Montreal to rent for ten people. My father is saving money for us, though." She was shaking the sand out of her sweater. "He's coming for a visit next month. I can't wait. He'll bring me some books. Maybe a new dress or a skirt. My father can actually buy clothes for a woman. He buys all my mother's clothes. Not many men can do that."

I felt chastened by her story. Wanted to compliment her. "Your English is really good."

She looked at me as if I'd insulted her, and of course I had. I'd patronized her with my remark, though I hadn't meant to. "I speak good English," she said, "because my father taught me. I also speak good French, but my father says that you need English to get ahead. The English run things in Quebec. They run the banks and the railways and the big stores, Eaton's, Simpson's, Morgan's. You have a better chance if you speak

English . . ." She stopped and then said, "My father is an interesting man. I am very proud of him. He speaks English, French, and Latin. He learned his Latin in a seminary. Are you a Catholic?"

I shook my head.

"I didn't think so," she said. "Most English people aren't Catholic. That's why they own everything, my father says. He has no love for the Church any more. I'm the only one he talks to about it, and it makes my mother mad because she's very devout. You can see that for yourself when she takes my brothers and sisters off to Mass every Sunday. I work on Sundays, but I still go to Mass when I can, but I'm more like my father than my mother. My father was going to be a priest, but he quit. He told me it didn't work for him. He didn't like what he was being told. He liked to read books too, and there were a lot of books that he was not allowed to read and he didn't think that was right. Books on religion and science and philosophy. My father is interested in all that stuff, and they wouldn't let him read about it, so he quit. And his mother and father, his brothers and sisters, none of them will speak to him now. The whole family is against him." She was leaning forward, hugging her knees again and rocking a little. "It will be good to see him and have a talk. It opens up my brain when I talk to him."

It was hot by then on the sand. We looked out to sea and watched the clouds moving in from the southwest. Farther down the beach we could see children playing under the railway bridge where the water was warmer. The big iron bridge above the children crossed a river to the sandbar that formed a natural barrier between the sea and the lagoon, a large tidal pond where seabirds rested and fed on little islands of marsh grass. On the seaward side of the bar was a long crescent of beach that stretched around the bay almost to the village of Percé.

Odette stopped gazing at the children and looked at me. "You should go and see Gabriel," she said. "He needs a friend for the summer and so do you. The boy is in a wheelchair. It wouldn't be any skin off your face to take him out and have a look at the girls and the tourists, would it? That mother of his is too busy with her friends, playing their card game. What do you call it? Bridges?"

"Bridge," I said. "Singular, and the expression in English is 'skin off your nose.'"

"Oh, yeah?" she said. "Well then, it would not be any skin off your big nose to be a friend to that boy. And you need a friend too, Mister Sorehead. You can't stay inside Madame La Plotte's house all summer."

"Please don't call me that," I said.

"What?"

"Mister Sorehead."

"You don't have much humour in you."

"I don't like to be made fun of, no."

"I'm only teasing you. Don't take it so tough."

"Hard," I said. "Don't take it so hard."

"Okay. Don't take it so hard."

I shrugged again. She was right. I took myself too seriously, and if I wanted to be this close to her, I would have to learn to parry her mocking remarks and adjust to her offhand manner. I didn't know how to talk to a girl, but I vowed I would learn.

I knew sitting next to her on the beach that day that I would never be her boyfriend. I was too young, too callow for her; I had already been relegated to the role of harmless eunuch, the platonic friend, the younger kid who just hangs around sniffing. But it was better than nothing. Being close to her like that I could still enjoy her slightly rank smell, the sight of a mole on her not-quite-clean neck, and that cast in her hazel eye, the sand between her toes.

As we started back along the shore, she was carrying her shoes and socks and sweater. Walking slightly behind her, I could admire how her feet in the sand lent a shapeliness to her pale calves. I asked her why she called Mrs. Moore, Madame Something-or-other.

"Madame La Plotte," she said. "The old bag doesn't like us. She thinks we're just a bunch of ignorant French Canadians with too many kids under one roof. We're always running around the house yelling at each other. She thinks she's better than us, but I'll bet she hasn't read as many books as my father, goddamn her eyes."

"But what does the word mean?" I asked.

Laughing, she turned around and began to walk backward. "What does it mean? I don't think you're old enough to know that."

I sprang forward and pushed her, the schoolyard impulse of a fourteen-year-old boy who feels challenged or insulted, even in jest, and I regretted it the moment I touched her. She stumbled back and fell. "I'm sorry," I said, reaching down for her. "I didn't mean it." But as she was getting up, she knocked my hand away.

"What a bully you are for your age, already beating up girls." I must have looked contrite enough, because she laughed. "Forget it. If I really felt like doing something, I would kick you in the balls. Just see if I wouldn't."

"You can kick me," I said, "but not there, please." We both laughed at that and I felt a rush of exhilaration, for I knew we were going to be friends. I had picked up her shoes and was knocking the sand out of them.

"Tell your uncle," Odette said, "that you want to go to Percé with him this afternoon. Tell him that you want to see Gabriel again. That you want to be his friend."

"He already has a friend," I said. "He has you."

"Me?" she said. "A friend?"

"Sure, he told me you were pretty good friends."

"He did, eh? Well, that's his opinion. We kid around when I'm cleaning his room. But don't forget that I'm cleaning his room. That's not what friends do. That's what people like me do. People like me are just servants to Gabriel and his mother. And to you and your uncle if you were staying at the St. Lawrence Hotel. You're all rich."

I wanted to say that I wasn't rich, that the rich were in another camp where I didn't belong or want to be. But I had come to Gaspé from Ontario by train in a sleeping compartment reserved for me by my father. My uncle wrote books and played tennis and bridge and drove a car. I went to a fancy school like Gabriel's. I badly wanted to be on her side, but how could I? That morning I had to settle for the notion that at least I had established a *beachhead*, a word I learned from reading the newspapers in the Groveland library after D-Day.

However goofy and maladroit Odette Huard thought I was, there had been contact between us, and I was prepared to move forward. I was discovering that you had to press forward with girls. You had to indicate your interest. Before we parted I said something about walking together again on another Monday. She was probably no more than amused by my suggestion and said only, "Sure," or "If you like."

After lunch that day I went to see my uncle to break the sullen week-long silence into which we had fallen. We had even taken to eating at different times to avoid each other. As soon as I heard his footsteps coming up the stairs and the closing of his study door, I would go down to the dining room. Mrs. Moore seemed resigned to this odd behaviour, and though it must have been a nuisance for her, she didn't say anything, at least to me. But that Monday I went to see my uncle in his room, where he spent an hour after lunch reading his day's work, smoking his pipe and chuckling over the antics of Billy and his pals. When I knocked on his door, he sounded distinctly headmasterish.

"Come," he called.

As I entered, he was staring at me over his reading glasses with the weary look of one who has endured the silence and emerged victorious, but who will now at least consider the entreaties of the vanquished. He waited for me to speak.

"Are you going to Percé this afternoon?" I asked.

"No, as a matter of fact, I'm not," he said. "I'm going up to Gaspé to have the car looked at. Why do you ask?"

"Well, next time you go to Percé, I'd like to come along."

He looked at me for what seemed like a long time, though

it was probably only a few moments. "Come to our senses, have we?"

"Yes," I said, "we have."

The next day, I went with him. A thunderstorm was passing over the hills and it was rainy and grey. The wipers on the little Willys didn't work properly, and Uncle Chester was almost climbing over the steering wheel to see as we rounded curves past the white pickets that separated the gravel highway from the steep ravines. I tried not to look, but stared at my uncle's head, which was grazing the car's roof as he peered through the windshield.

At the St. Lawrence Hotel, Mrs. Fontaine was delighted to see me and I got an extravagant hug. I came from people who were not physically demonstrative and so to be embraced so ardently by a lovely woman was deliciously mystifying.

"It's so good to see you again, James," she said. "Gabriel's been asking about you. He's in his room. Go up and see him."

I found him listening to music on the phonograph. I had heard it from time to time on the radio at home. I didn't know the name of it then, but I'm sure now it was from Ferde Grofé's *Grand Canyon Suite*. I thought it was very highbrow stuff at the time. Gabriel looked pleased with himself as he wheeled his chair away from the window where he'd been looking out at something through a pair of binoculars.

"I've got something to tell you," he said. Those were his first words to me that day. No "Hello" or "How are you?" Just "I've got something to tell you." As if I'd only been gone for twenty minutes and was just dropping by again.

"And what's that?" I asked, trying to sound like someone

above the fray who is nevertheless mildly amused by the romantic entanglements of others, for I had a good idea what he wanted to talk about.

"On Saturday I got pretty close," he said.

"What are you talking about?"

"The girl, the girl," he said. "The little French chambermaid. I nearly got in."

I could no longer help myself. "What happened?"

"I was still in my pyjamas when the two of them came to the door. I had planned it that way. So I said, 'Go ahead, don't mind me.' Odette and I have this little game and the chubby one knows and plays along. After they do most of the cleaning stuff, Pauline goes out to start another room and Odette stays here to finish up. We've been kissing and stuff now for a couple of weeks, and when she's making the bed, she lets me feel her up a bit. I'll say, 'How about a little kiss, Odette?' and she'll say 'Okay.' But on Saturday morning I pulled her down onto me and asked her to sit on my lap. Just for a minute. Oh, I had such a boner on, James. She must have felt it there beneath her. So we started kissing and things got pretty hot, I can tell you. I had my hand under her dress, but she grabbed my wrist. Brother, it was so frustrating. Then she had to leave. But I'm nearly there, James, I can feel it. I'm going to get in this week. I've got my rubbers handy."

Rubbers? He had rubbers? I had only seen such things used playfully. A boy I knew once brought some back to the school after a vacation. Said he stole them from a drawer in his father's dresser. We filled them with water and swung those great sacks in the communal shower, where they would often burst

agreeably across someone's hindquarters. But I knew that was
a long way from how they were meant to be used. Was Gabriel
only adorning his prurient tale to impress me? The way he
described things *did* sound convincing. I could picture Odette
sitting on his lap while he groped her. Yes, I could see it all
clearly in my mind's eye. Of course I didn't mention to Gabriel
that I had spent the previous morning with her and that she
had given me a slightly different version of what transpired in
his room. There is a furtive side to me. I enjoy listening to the
secrets of others, and over the years people have opened their
hearts to me. This trait has made me seem more trustworthy
than I really am. In my former life as a professor, it proved a
valuable gift, often enabling me to be privy to what was really
going on within the interstices of academic politics; helping
me to solidify friendships, or what passes for them in university life, keeping enemies wary and fearful. Looking back on
it all now, I am filled with a vague distaste for this inclination of mine. It seems now to have been such a waste of time.
Catherine Parmeter once told me that I would have made a
perfect Renaissance courtier.

"Someone like Osric, you mean?" I said to her.

"Well, no, not Osric," she said. "Osric is a comedic figure,
Shakespeare's parody of an Elizabethan yes-man. I was thinking of someone more serious, someone intelligent enough,
but not particularly ambitious, even a bit lazy, happy enough
to be out of the spotlight; someone who can keep his mouth
shut, listen to both sides and offer the king wise counsel."

"A devious sneak, then," I said. "Historically such people
often lost their heads."

"But organizations need them," she said. "Courts, corporations, universities, government bureaucracies. They need people like you."

"And we no longer lose our heads?"

"Not strictly speaking, no."

Not an especially flattering picture of me, but it's how I'm made, and that day in Gabriel Fontaine's room, I was trying to balance his account of events with what Odette had told me. The pointless speculations of the lovelorn bystander. I think that was the day Gabriel loaned me his new binoculars, a recent gift from his father in Washington. Gabriel knew that I was far more interested in the war than he was, and he said I could now look seriously for U-boats. But I really wanted the binoculars so that I could observe Odette at unguarded moments. I wanted to watch her sitting on the gallery, leaning forward to cut her toenails. I wanted to focus the lens on that mole on her neck just behind her right ear. I wanted to study her knees when she hitched up her dress for a little sun on those shapely, pale legs. The binoculars would help.

It was unlike me to change plans, and my family knew this, so it was important that I let them know about Switzerland. When I returned that Friday night to my hotel room I sat on the bed for quite some time thinking about it. I had to tell my children. But what could I say? That I was going to Zurich to be with a man I hadn't seen in sixty years who intended to end his life? It sounded too bizarre. Didn't we already have enough morbidity to deal with? Had Catherine Parmeter still been in my life, I could have told her everything. I imagined her raised eyebrows. "James, what on earth . . . ?" Euthanasia wouldn't sit well with Catherine's beliefs. We must see it all through to the bitter end. Life is sacred and so on. David might not be unduly troubled by the truth. "Sure, Dad, why not? Another couple of days? I take it your friend's paying for it all?" David's accounting mentality owes unyielding allegiance to the famous bottom line. But I couldn't possibly tell Susan the entire story. It would be easier to dissemble. My old acquaintance was rich, lonely, and bored. He needed company. Which, when I thought of it, was not all that far from the truth.

It was still fairly early in the evening, perhaps nine-thirty, when I called Susan and told her. She sounded, as I had expected, surprised. "How extraordinary. And after sixty years you recognized this man?"

"I did, yes. Still in a wheelchair of course and the face old and lined. Gabriel is far from well, but I could still see the boy I once knew in an old man's face."

"Why Switzerland, Dad? I'm told it's rather dull. I can't imagine you'll be skiing."

"No, skiing is not on the agenda."

"Too bad he couldn't have asked you along to Italy or France. Take in the grape harvest or something."

The slightly mocking tone in her voice was a passageway into our old joking zone. "When I think of Switzerland," she said, "I think of that movie. I'm sure we've watched it together on television. *The Third Man*."

"Yes. Written by Graham Greene."

"That's the one. Remember the scene in the Ferris wheel where the Orson Welles character is rationalizing his outrageous conduct in the black market by implying that evil has always been around. He cites Renaissance Italy and the Borgias and suggests that out of that corrupt civilization with all its wars and troubles came great art. As for Switzerland, he says, they had five hundred years of peace and what did that produce?"

We actually said it together as we laughed. "The cuckoo clock."

"A bit hard on the poor old Swiss," I said.

"Anyway, good for you, Dad." Then she surprised me by saying exactly what I had anticipated David saying. "I assume your friend is paying for everything."

"Yes. Money, it seems, is no problem for Gabriel."

"Well, good then. Give me a call when you get back to Toronto next week. About five is best. I'm still in my office then. That's noon your time."

"How are you feeling?" I imagined she would grow exceedingly tired of that question in the months ahead. Perhaps she already was, but I had to ask.

"About the same, Dad. Nothing's changed. I feel fine right now. A little tired maybe. I told Esther last night, by the way. I asked her over for a drink. She's been wonderful. We agreed that I'll address the school on Monday at assembly. Tell them what needs to be said. That I'm ill and that I'm taking a leave of absence. I won't go into details. Just put the students and faculty in the picture. I've already talked to the chair of the board and she's been great too. She is going to tell the others at a meeting early in the week."

"Have you thought any more about treatment?"

"I've thought about it. Sophie's been looking into hospice care for me too. It's beginning to look as if the most sensible approach is for me to return to Toronto. Just when that will be, I don't know. I'll wait until after the surgery. I just don't know yet."

"Of course you don't. A day at a time."

Susan sounded almost buoyant and perhaps that is what happens. A door opens just a crack. A glimmer of light in a dark room. Or is it just sharing your news with others? Learning to live with it. To be followed no doubt by periods of despair. But others now knew and wanted to help in whatever way they could, and that at least was something.

"Have a good time in dull old Switzerland, Dad. At least spend some of your rich friend's money."

"I'll do my best."

It felt strange, my not having told her the reason for the journey, and when I hung up the phone, I felt stranded sitting there on my bed in the Edward Lear Hotel on Seymour Street. I knew that not telling Susan the exact truth was in her best interests, but we have always tried to be honest with each other, hence my uneasiness. It was then nearly five in Toronto, probably too late to reach David, who leaves the office early on Fridays, but I tried anyway and was told by his secretary that he had indeed left for the weekend. So I called his home number. Home is now a condominium at the foot of Bay Street overlooking Lake Ontario. He shares this space with Nikki Martin, who is twenty-eight and works in advertising. No one in the living flesh answered, but I did get to listen to what is surely one of the sexiest voices in the western hemisphere. "Hi. You've reached Nikki and David. Neither of us is available at the moment. Please leave a message and we'll get back to you. Have a really super day." I left a message.

Next was my daughter-in-law Brenda, whom I'm fond of, though her marinated bitterness often wears me out. Brenda has been badly hurt, no question about that, and for the most part, I'm sympathetic. In the first years of her marriage to David, Brenda used to flirt with me in an innocent way and

I suppose I was flattered by the attention. She may have just felt sorry for me, a lonely but still presentable widower. In any case, she set out to win me over and she did. She was pregnant when David married her and mistakenly believed that I viewed the whole arrangement as ill advised and precipitate. In fact, I was delighted for both of them and saw in Brenda a settling influence on my son. But she seemed to harbour fears that she would not be accepted into our family and so was determined to be a loving wife and daughter-in-law. She was in awe of Susan and badly wanted her approval, which she quickly got. Susan also happens to like her sister-in-law very much.

Brenda is a nurse and has, I think, an exaggerated respect for so-called educated people. She's a tough-minded woman who didn't have it easy early in life: a difficult childhood in a small northern town, shunted between a single mother and grandparents. She moved to Toronto on her own and worked as a waitress in a cocktail bar to put herself through a nursing program. She built a life out of very little, and I admired her for it. She met my son when he was in hospital for an appendectomy. She was sexy and animated, and David, whom I always saw perhaps unfairly as rather priggish, must have been entranced by the idea of having that spectacular body all to himself.

After Gillian was born, Brenda asked me for a list of books to read. She felt she had missed out on something and wanted to catch up. So I provided one, which she dutifully followed, though she seemed reluctant to talk about any of the books. It was as if reading them was enough. At one point I suggested that she enroll in a night course at the university. Get some feedback from others about what she was reading. So she did some survey course, Chaucer to Eliot or something. But it wasn't successful; she was either too impatient or simply bored, and her interest waned and then fizzled out. Brenda seems trapped by sudden enthusiasms and the need to know. But to know what? I once asked her. Just to know what educated people know, she said. I might have told her that if by "educated" she meant people who had spent a few years at university, then I would have to say not much. But I didn't. I wanted to encourage my touchy, defensive, and immensely likeable daughter-in-law, who now, on the cusp of forty, lived in a comfortable house on Melrose Avenue in what used to be called North Toronto with a beautiful sulky teenage daughter and a twelve-year-old son.

Brenda wasn't at home either. Instead I got my grandson, Brian, who in some ways reminds me of myself at that age but who may even be a little more peculiar than I was then. Despite his secretive nature, Brian once told me at length of his strange fears. For a while he explored Web sites devoted to unsettling tales of children afflicted with rare misfortunes. He told me, for instance, of a boy his age who suffered a stroke that left him blind, deaf, dumb, and paralyzed. Brian wondered how anyone could live like that. Another child had horrifying lesions over his entire body. His skin could scarcely tolerate the lightest covering. Yet another had no throat and was fed intravenously. One day Brian asked me what it felt like to be old, and I told him that your body creaked and ached. You also snored and farted a lot. And that of course convulsed him with laughter. I joined in too, both of us filled with mirth at the thought of so much farting. But overall he is a serious boy, small for his age, watchful and bewildered by his father's decision to live elsewhere. For the time being, it looks as if Brian has decided that the adult world is too complicated to approach, and so he spends hours on the computer in his bedroom annihilating hordes of aliens. I have watched him at this pursuit, amazed at his dexterity as he saves our planet.

I was soon listening to his breathy little voice. "Hello, Grandpa, I thought you were in England."

"I am, Brian."

I could hear the throb of rap music and chanting in the background. Gillian and her new boyfriend, Jermaine Clifford, were probably upstairs listening to this stuff. Jermaine and his baggy pants and assorted jewellery. He's worked on his rap artist glare and I think enjoys presenting this threatening image to white folks. But I suspect that it's all a pose; he can't even claim the current distinction in rap culture of being born poor with street smarts denied to middle-class kids. His mother is a professor of sociology and his father works for the city. Gillian told me that Jermaine's grades at Lawrence Park are in the eighties. He is clearly university bound. Yet Brenda is having a great deal of difficulty with the idea of her daughter having a black boyfriend.

"How are you doing, Grandpa?" Brian asked. "How's Aunt Susan?"

"I'm okay, but your aunt is not well, I'm afraid."

"Is she going to die, Grandpa?"

"We don't know that yet, Brian. We have to wait for more tests. She will be well looked after."

"That's good. Mom's not here now. Just Gillian and Jermaine. Mom's across the street at Mrs. Taylor's."

"That's okay. Just tell her that I'll call again on Sunday. Tell her there's been a change in my plans. I've met an old friend and I'm going with him to Switzerland for a couple of days. Can you remember that?"

"Sure I can, Grandpa."

I have always been amused by Brian's matter-of-fact manner and his guarded interest in the life of adults. He was in the back seat of his father's car when David drove me to the airport on the Saturday after Susan's call, looking like some small important figure, the son of a Middle Eastern prince, say, with his dark eyes and the olive-coloured skin that both he and his father inherited from my late wife, who was Jewish. Without seeming to, Brian was listening to what was going on. I had wanted to take the limousine service; at such times I enjoy the tidiness of being by myself and the impersonal politeness of the driver, who, if you so wish, will leave you alone with your thoughts. And my thoughts of course were on Susan. But David insisted and arrived at my apartment building on Edmonds Avenue with the boy strapped into the back seat. They had spent the day together. Had gone to lunch and a movie, though I gathered that things had not been entirely successful.

As we drove up Avenue Road towards the freeway, I glanced sideways at my son's aggrieved profile. A good-looking man with some of the dapper handsomeness of J. T. Hillyer, whom David resembles in temperament. As a teenager, he was spindly and sullen, and after his mother's death he seemed to waste away. I was frightened for his health but powerless to do anything about it. He appeared to resent the fact that I was still breathing and his mother wasn't. For a couple of years, we had a bad time of it, David and I. Mostly from spite, I think, he dropped out of university and lived in various arrangements with other unmoored souls in lofts and apartments around town. He was affectless in a maddening way, working in video stores or delivering pizza, smoking, I imagine, a lot of cannabis. He was painfully thin, intense, fanatical. He looked like a young Jesuit, and for a while he was interested in Scientology. I would take him out on a Sunday and watch him wolf down roast beef and mashed potatoes. We hardly exchanged a word during these meals. Susan too would have him over to her place. She was more successful in listening and talking to him. I had no patience with his aimlessness and his goofy religion—and perhaps, as Dr. Schumann told him during a lengthy and no doubt expensive consultation in the midst of his marital upheaval twenty years later, I failed him in important ways during that time when he was, to use the psychiatrist's words, "searching for himself after the loss of his mother." Or so he told me not so long ago. In any case, it was a bleak period in both our lives, and I understand naturally that David was always closer to his mother than he was to me and that her death affected him deeply. Then abruptly, as if awakening from a long sleep well-rested and alert, he got down to business. Came to me one day and said he wanted to go back to university. And so he did. He became a successful accountant and within what seemed like just a few years, a fairly wealthy man. Still, David remains cranky.

On the way to the airport he complained bitterly about his daughter. "I don't know about that guy she's seeing now. Don't get me wrong, Dad, I've got nothing against African-Canadians, but I just don't like him. He's always carrying this big attitude. He looks at you as if you're an obstacle to get by."

I suggested that Jermaine Clifford was probably not as dangerous as he looked, but right now it was dress-up time and he was acting out a role, just like millions of other young people, black, brown, white, or yellow. Didn't David remember how moody and obstinate he was as a teenager? I was trying to get a rise out of him, and at one point, seeking complicity, I turned to the grave little figure with the seat belt strapped across his chest. Brian appeared to be engrossed in his electronic game, but he glanced up with a look that said *this is interesting*. I wanted the boy to imagine his father as a seventeen-year-old pain in the ass.

We were then in the outside lane of the big highway, travelling westward, the sun obscured behind a bank of clouds, the rays spilling across the sky. David is a fast, aggressive driver who can't bear to have anyone in front of him, and his car is a large silver something-or-other. Intregal. Intergal. Integrity. Surely not, but what crazy names for cars nowadays! In any case, we were seated on black leather with Pachelbel's *Canon* on the sound system and I was trying to listen to my son, but I was also nervous about how close David was to the car ahead, which would not move over. I could see no driver, just the headrest. Then a spray of rear lights and I held my breath as David braked smoothly and the big car stopped a few feet behind the headless driver. David hadn't missed a beat in his diatribe.

"Gill's grades are way down too. If she wants to get into a good university, she'd better pull up her socks."

I must have smiled at this old expression. How quickly David had gone from feckless youth to sanctimonious adult. And he was only, what? Forty-two.

"I don't know how Brenda puts up with her. I have to give her credit. You should hear the way that girl talks to her mother, Dad."

In fact I had overheard some of these outbursts—but what was the point in confirming anything? David had to get it all out of his system. It was the price I was paying for the ride. I only wished he had shown a little more brotherly regard for his sister's condition, though as he neared the airport he did ask about health care in the U.K. It had to be better than ours with its long waiting lists, et cetera, et cetera. What about the States? Had she thought about that? Expensive of course, but efficient. Shouldn't we look into it?

"If it's a question of money, Dad, tell Sue not to worry about it. I'll be glad to help."

This was true. David would never see anyone close to him suffer from lack of money.

In front of Arrivals, he told me to convey his best to Susan and tell her to consider treatment in the States. David admires America. Likes its pushy foreign policy and its low taxes. He and Nikki have talked about moving there one day, and it wouldn't surprise me to see them end up in someplace like Colorado Springs or San Diego. As I was getting out of the car, David looked back at his son.

"Do you want to sit in the front now, Brian?"

"No thanks, Dad." And so he remained there, waving solemnly to me as they drove off.

After talking to Brian on the telephone, I lay awake thinking of Gabriel Fontaine in his bed a few blocks south of me. The next morning he was going to drive around London attempting to recreate a day in the summer of 1938, looking out another car window, trying to recall what he had seen as a ten-year-old boy with his mother and father. How the bobby with the tall helmet had rerouted them because of the black-shirted demonstrators. I was eight years old in 1938, and while Gabriel and his parents were being driven around London, I may have been sitting on the front steps of the house on Crescent Road in my short pants and white shirt, waiting for my parents to take me to church. We drove to St. Paul's on Bloor Street, and I went off to Sunday school and pasted another picture of Jesus and his disciples into an attendance book. From the open window, I probably heard the congregation singing. *Praise my soul, the King of Heaven / To his feet, thy tribute bring.*

I lay in bed in the Edward Lear Hotel that Friday night trying to imagine Gabriel in the black car all those years ago, looking out at the demonstrators and the thin pale Londoners lining the streets. A healthy good-looking American boy with perfect teeth, his hair carefully combed. Beside him the beautiful young mother attending to his every need, and his father, an older presence and source of all the bounty, looking out with approving eyes at Mosley's supporters. Later the family might take a ride on the Thames to the Tower of London and Greenwich. A lovely late afternoon on the river, only a few weeks before Prime Minister Chamberlain flew off to Munich in his striped trousers to meet Herr Hitler. It was the summer before Gabriel contracted polio. The happiest day of his life. And now he wanted a final look at what he thought he remembered of that day.

On Mondays Odette and I walked along the cliffside and down the little path to the cove. Or across the railway bridge to the sandbar and the long beach that curved around the shore towards Percé. There we carried our shoes and walked barefoot on the hard damp sand. Odette liked me, I could tell. I was younger than Gabriel and quieter, patient, a good listener. Perhaps I was just more restful to be around. We talked about our families and schools. She made up funny names for the nuns who taught her in the village school. There was the Beast, who was ugly with warts on her chin. When she was in a bad mood, she pulled your hair or twisted your ear for no good reason. Just to be mean, Odette said. There was Mrs. Christ, who was young and plain and impossibly pious, her hands pointed upward in prayer even when she recited the multiplication tables. And the Milkwagon, who was short and fat with the biggest tits on the Gaspé coast. I laughed, but I was shocked too. I didn't think girls talked like that.

For the rest of the week, while my uncle played bridge with Mrs. Fontaine and the Porters, I was Gabriel's companion, his dogsbody, perhaps his friend. I was never completely certain of that. It always seemed to me that his wise-cracking, all-knowing manner left little room for genuine feeling; that I was merely an audience for his daily accounting of Odette Huard's seduction. And then one day, he told me he was in. It had happened that morning he said. They both got carried away and he got in. And it wasn't her first time either, he said. While they were at it, Odette's friend Pauline had stood guard like Juliet's nurse in the hallway.

He told me this while he poured rum into my bottle of Coca-Cola. He had bartered for a mickey of Captain Morgan from one of the waiters in the bar after they came to some agreement involving American cigarettes. That day I remember there was a party for the Porters, who were celebrating an anniversary. They were all in the dining room having a boozy lunch, according to Gabriel, who thought we had plenty of time for drinks of our own. I had never tasted alcohol, but I was eager enough to get drunk. I wanted to cover my ears as I listened to details of that morning. Either that or take the window blind cord and tighten it around Gabriel's neck while he talked. In a lifetime there are afternoons you must live through during which you listen to people who believe that you are on their side. And so it was with Gabriel and me that day. While he talked, I drank greedily, and of course I drank too much and later was sick in the bathroom. I seem to remember putting my head out the little window with its frosted glass and braying like a donkey, either from revulsion at his tale, or from sheer happiness at being drunk. Gabriel was laughing as he pulled me back and gave me a package of Sens-Sens, a cheap breath freshener of the day. I fell asleep on his bed, and at one point awakened to hear him talking to his mother, who was at the door. She had brought up some cake from the luncheon party for us. I don't know how he explained my lying on his bed or even how he got rid of her, because I went back to sleep.

When I woke up, he gave me aspirin and two or three glasses of water. He was apologetic. "It's my fault, James. It happens to the best of us. Your first time, I suppose?"

"Not really."

He ignored the lie and got right to the point. Typically Gabriel. He was beside himself with excitement. Always a bad sign. "Listen, James, I have a plan. Since yesterday I have been thinking about what to do."

"To do? To do what?"

"To screw Odette of course. What else?" Wheeling the chair over to the window he got his cigarettes from the ledge, and after firing up a Camel, he pushed himself back towards me. "We were lucky this morning," he said, "but chances are that sooner or later Mother is going to pop in on us and that could be embarrassing. Pauline can't watch everything."

I have an image of myself sitting on the edge of the bed listening to all this, dazed and probably still a little drunk.

"I've got an idea, though," said Gabriel, "but I'm going to need your help."

"My help?"

"Yes, old boy, your help."

While I was sleeping, he had been thinking of a place where he and Odette could have sex, and he'd discovered, in the corridor leading to the service elevator, a large closet used by the maids to store dust mops and vacuum cleaners. With a little work, a space could be cleared, just enough to fit in a mattress and the wheelchair. "It was there all the time," he said. "Right under my nose."

It was then that I noticed how the palms of his hands were shiny and reddened. He would almost certainly have blisters the next day. Apparently he had wheeled himself down the hallway, opened the door, manoeuvred his chair into the corridor and inspected this closet. I had to admire his determination. What he had in mind was for me to wheel him away in the afternoons as usual in full view of the others, out of the hotel and onto the main street. But instead of going to the wharf, we would turn around and return to the hotel, going past the kitchen to the little service elevator and up to the corridor and this refurbished love bower. My next duty, he said, would be to stand guard by the elevator in case someone from the maintenance staff might use it. But it was unlikely, he said. "Once in a blue moon" was, I believe, the phrase he used. He then assured me that this would only be two or three times a week. And it wouldn't take long. Fifteen or twenty minutes at the most. Pauline would continue to patrol the hallway while I played the role of Friar Lawrence in the corridor. These references to *Romeo and Juliet* come to mind because of a school production that year at Groveland. Boys' schools used to love putting on plays that allowed for cross-dressing, and I remember how we all enjoyed watching the quarterback of the football team present himself as a ravishing Juliet.

"And what," I asked, "if, while I'm standing 'guard,' someone uses the elevator? Perhaps that 'once-in-a-blue moon person'?"

"Then," said Gabriel, smiling, "you come along and knock on the door. Maybe two long and one short. Like Morse code. We'll work out a system of signals. So when we hear the signal, we'll be quiet and you can go out to the hallway and pass the time of day with Pauline. Nobody will see anything amiss in you standing there talking to her."

"But," I said, "the person coming up in the service elevator might find something 'amiss,' as you put it, if she opens the closet door and sees you and Odette."

"It won't happen. Don't be such a worrywart."

"I'm not worried. It's not my funeral if you're caught."

"We won't get caught."

"And suppose I meet your mother in the hall? Suppose she's coming up from a card game with another piece of cake for the young prince? What will she make of things? Here is James and a little French-Canadian girl. But where is my beloved son Gabriel? What should I tell her? That he's screwing the other maid in the broom closet?"

Gabriel was frowning. He didn't care at all for this sarcastic persona I had suddenly adopted; it didn't square with his notion of my role as the doltish but willing sidekick.

"All right, it's risky," he said, "but nothing ventured, nothing gained. And when you really think of it, what are the odds of something like that happening? Of someone coming up in the service elevator at the same time as the mater is climbing the stairs and meeting you in the hallway? You know how they play bridge every day from two to five. It's almost religious."

"Yes," I said, "but you can't deny that it might happen."

Then, a mistake on my part as I appealed to his sense of right and wrong. A fool's errand, as it turned out. I should have known better. "Suppose," I said, "that you're caught?"

Another frown. Gabriel wasn't used to being cross-examined and there was now a hint of resentment in his voice. "Well, suppose we are."

"Well, think about it, Gabriel," I said. "It may turn out all right for you. A lecture from your mother. A bit of finger wagging. But what about the girl? She'll lose her job."

I could see from his uncomprehending look that I had gone down the wrong road. Gabriel had no idea what Odette's life outside the St. Lawrence Hotel was really like, and moreover he probably didn't want to know. Still the jealous young prig soldiered on.

"She lives in the house next door to my uncle and me. It's a big family. Ten or twelve children, I think. She probably helps out with her wages. But they'll fire her for sure, Gabriel. She'll be out the door. She'll be talked about around that village. It'll all get back to her mother. To the village priest. There's no father in the house, you know." Technically, that was true, though I was hoping to convey the impression that she had no father. Another mistake.

"She's told me about her father," Gabriel said. "He works in a munitions factory in Montreal and makes pretty good money. Those guys rake it in with overtime. Anyway, they're not going to be in that village for long. She told me they might even move back to Montreal at the end of the summer. Her father is looking for a place for them. Listen, James, that girl has been around. She knows the score."

"All right, all right, she knows the score," I said.

It was a measure of Gabriel's incuriosity about the lives of others, including mine, that not for a moment did he imagine that my acidic objections to his cockamamie scheme came from any interest on my part in Odette Huard. I threw down my last desperate card. "You don't even like her much," I said.

"That's not true," he said, lighting another cigarette and sipping more rum and Coke, none of which seemed to affect him unduly. "I like Odette," he said. "She's no beauty with that wandering eye of hers, but she's got a great body. She's pretty smart too in her own way."

"Well, I'm not sure I want to go along with this," I said. "Why should I anyway?"

For the first time he looked both incredulous and offended. "Why should you?" he asked. "Why, because we're pals of course."

And so we were, at least in his mind. How could I fail to see how he looked at things? I had met any number of self-centred boys at Groveland, but Gabriel was exceptional. He was fixed solely on himself and his need to be in charge. To use a word popular in the first half of the old century, Gabriel had *drive*, a vigorous and ambitious need to assert his will on others. A concomitant of this *drive* was the expectation that others existed solely to do his bidding. Without his warmth and enthusiasm, his generosity and good humour—all of which could be assembled under the rubric of *charm*—Gabriel would have been merely repellent, a monster of solipsism.

None of his *charm*, however, kept him from being touchy. I remember how he wheeled himself back across the room to the window, and sat there looking out and smoking, offering me his profile and addressing his remarks to the outdoors.

"I don't know why you made that wisecrack about my mother and the piece of cake, James. And you called me a young prince or something. Well, I'll just say this, pal. My life these past few years hasn't made me feel much like a prince."

Words! O glorious words! Words that arrive on time to succour and redeem the lives of the also-rans. Over the years I'd learned that witty remarks could disarm bullies and win the admiration of others more favoured by looks and popularity. At Groveland, words had saved me from various wallopings and humiliations. In later years my admittedly sarcastic tongue would infuriate faculty enemies, delight adept students, and confound dullards. And that afternoon in the St. Lawrence Hotel, my words had reduced Gabriel Fontaine to whining, which I felt did not become him. A disappointment. I had expected better. So a small but genuine victory for me, his pal.

"Fifteen or twenty minutes of your time, twice a week," he said. "Is that such a big deal?"

I told him I'd think about it.

Behind my carefully managed pose of insouciance, however, I was in a jealous fury, and the next day I told Uncle Chester that I didn't feel well enough to go to Percé. He seemed peevish himself, informing me that he intended to spend the afternoon catching up on his correspondence, adding that I myself might display a little consideration by writing my mother, who, if it had escaped my attention, had been writing faithfully to me each week. Somewhat chastened, I went to my attic room, where I reread my mother's latest letter before replying. The business about her writing each week was not true; her letters tended to arrive haphazardly, at the beck and call of her fancy. It was the same at school. For weeks I never gave Mother a thought, and then I would get a letter every day for a spell, each in its own way a quirky commentary on the world around her. Looked at in a certain light, they could easily have been seen as the handiwork of a mild crackpot. I chose, however, not to regard them that way; I was always grateful for her rather skewed take on things.

In her last letter she had mentioned a visit to her psychiatrist in a big red building on Queen Street. Aunt Margery waited for her in the family Buick, smoking cigarettes and reading the *Saturday Evening Post*, watching the inmates as they strolled among the trees talking to themselves and making faces. Aunt Margery was fascinated by mental illness and envied Mother the opportunity to be psychoanalyzed. Whenever Susan and I watched a video of Hitchcock's 1945 corny melodrama, *Spellbound*, with Ingrid Bergman and Gregory Peck as two psychiatrists, we always referred to it as "Aunt Margery's movie," for it was certainly her all-time favourite.

Mother described Dr. Peterson as small and precise—"a rather dainty little man" was how she put it. He asked her a great many questions about her childhood. Had she ever dreamt of killing her parents? Had she been jealous of her sister and brother? Had she ever dreamt of killing *them?* He went on endlessly about her dreams, which she confessed to me she began to make up, embellishing them with lurid and outrageous details while she looked out his office window at Aunt Margery in the parking lot. Many years later when I read the autobiography of a famous novelist, I was delighted to discover that he too, bored by a psychiatrist's questions, had invented his dreams and presented them for interpretation. I underlined the particular passage and gave the book to my mother, who was then in a nursing home. After she'd read the book, she wrote me a witty thank-you note on very good stationery. It was the kind of thing those of her generation did.

In her letter to me back in 1944, she complained good-naturedly enough that Margery was being stingy with the five o'clock gin and tonics. She was to have only two small ones, on J. T.'s orders. As Mother said, "It seems a bit unfair in my own home." She asked me how I was getting along with her brother, reminding me that Chester's "bark was worse than his bite" and that he had only my best interests at heart. I didn't altogether believe that, but neither did I dismiss it. Dr. Peterson, she said, wanted to try electroshock therapy on her "to wake up my depression," but she was resisting the procedure. She closed by telling me to take care of myself and be a good boy. She also enclosed a two-dollar bill. I could see her writing these words in her small neat hand on the blue stationery she favoured, sitting at the desk in her little room late at night, the moths beating against the lighted windows that overlooked the garden. A far-off siren. The heavy dark night of summer in Toronto. I could get quite homesick reading one of Mother's letters.

The next Monday on my walk with Odette, I was carrying my purloined copy of Tennyson's poems, and Gabriel's binoculars, which I had no intention of giving back until he asked for them. Why was I carrying such things? To show Odette that some people have more serious interests in life than mere carnal pleasure. Let her and the rich American go at it; I was far too busy reading poetry or scanning the sea for German treachery. You never knew. Some malfunction in the boat's system for circulating air. The sailors gasping for oxygen as the captain sounds the alarm to surface. Then that insidious grey thing emerging right in the sightline of my field glasses. U-156. I saw myself running to Robin, Jones & Whitman to call the naval base at Sandy Beach. My picture in the newspapers across the land. There would be a ceremony at the school in the fall. When Odette asked me what I was looking at, I told her, but she didn't seem impressed, and shortly afterward, I picked up my Tennyson and began to read. I think it was "The Lotos-Eaters," for I knew the story. We'd studied *The Odyssey* at school.

Odette had brought along an old towel, grey and full of holes. I had never seen anything so tattered yet still in use. It was wrenching to see her sitting on it. I was watching her out of the corner of my eye, only pretending to read of course, punishing her with my silence. Hateful. I confess it now. My behaviour that day was hateful. I knew how much Odette had trouble with the corrosive silence that my uncle and I, for example, could endure for days, even weeks. But Odette couldn't bear it and would soon fall into either scolding or kidding until you relented. But that day with my binoculars and my book, she wasn't sure how to take me. All right, maybe there are Germans out there, so go ahead and look. As for reading, that was a serious endeavour. Odette liked reading. Earlier that week she had finished *Tobacco Road*. It had bored her in places, but she'd stuck with it, though she said she didn't like stories about poor people. "I see enough poor people around here," she said. She wanted something else to read, and I had thought of loaning her *Great Expectations*, but I was only halfway through and it had to last me the summer. So that day I had her slightly off balance with my binoculars and my book.

She had taken off her shoes and socks and was sitting on that awful towel with her legs apart, scooping up handfuls of sand like a child, watching it sift through her fingers, waiting for me to say something, though maybe not. Maybe she was thinking of Gabriel. I was thinking of them both. Entwined in sex. Those legs I saw outstretched in the sand had been around him. How had they managed it? How could she sit there looking so ...? But how did I expect her to look? Without glancing up, still playing with the sand, she asked me what I was reading and I told her.

"I know a poem," she said, brightening. "This English boy in Montreal told me this poem:

Jack and Jill went up the hill
To get a pail of water
They stayed a while
Behind a stile
And now they have a daughter."

She expected me to laugh, but I was too miserable. "What's a stile anyway?" she asked. "I never did find out. Some kind of shed?"

"I don't know," I said.

"Can I look at your book?"

I handed it to her and she began to turn the pages. "You should hear the Milkwagon read poetry. It's pretty funny with her accent. "De sun go down and over all / Dese barren reach by de tide." She sent me once to Mother Margaret Ann for laughing and I got a strapping. Six on each hand, goddamn her eyes."

I was looking through the binoculars.

"Can I keep this book for a while?" she asked.

"I guess so."

"Hey," she said, "I just remembered. I got some cigarettes. You want one?" She was digging in the pocket of her house-dress. "One of the tourists threw his package into the waste-basket and there were still four left in it. You'd be surprised what they throw away."

It was hard to light a cigarette in the wind and she told me to turn around to provide a shield. "Like this," she said, squaring my shoulders.

When she had lit her cigarette, she lit one for me off hers. I liked the way the wind lifted the hair off her neck as she sat there smoking. I had settled back on the sand and half closed my eyes, watching her.

After a while she said, "You smoke like a little kid, James. Like this, look."

The sunlight was burning through my eyelids, turning

everything a fiery orange, but I could see her blowing the smoke out in quick little puffs. It was true. I didn't know how to smoke. Didn't even enjoy it.

My moodiness was getting on her nerves. I could sense it when she mentioned Uncle Chester. There was an edge to her voice.

"He's a strange one, that uncle of yours. People think he's one of those queers."

I said nothing to that.

"That would be a good joke on Madame La Plotte. Thinking she is high above the rest of us and all the time keeping a queer man in her house." She was smiling down at me, leaning on an elbow. "Maybe the man is not even your uncle. Maybe you are his young friend."

I closed my eyes and was silent.

"I know you are listening to me, James. I hope you like girls. You are just at the age when you should be interested. My brothers Maurice and Raymond are horny all the time. I hear them at night," she laughed. "It's so funny to hear them at that. Wringing the chicken's neck and groaning away like anything."

I wondered then if she had seen me on that day by the cliffside.

"So what about that Mister Chester with his little moustache and his wavy hair that looks marcelled?"

I opened my eyes. "Marcelled?"

"Yes, you know. He must use the curling iron on that hair."

"Don't be silly, Odette," I said, closing my eyes again. "My uncle has naturally wavy hair. He just combs it."

"Oh sure," she said, sitting up again and hugging her knees.

She looked at me. "So? Is he funny, your uncle?"

"Funny?"

"Yes, you know. Does he like other men? Boys?"

I remember putting my hands behind my head and looking up at the travelling clouds, the grave young listener considering her question. "To tell you the truth, Odette, I don't really know." This answer had not only the virtue of being true, but also the appearance of sounding like it. The manner in which I had expressed my opinion—its truthful earnestness—clearly puzzled her, and surprised me as well. It had sounded rather grown up.

"'To tell you the truth,'" Odette repeated. "I have heard that expression from others. Mr. Cedric at Robin's uses it all the time."

I pictured the store manager in his smock and his striped shirt with the elastic sleeve bands, a nineteenth-century figure, climbing one of the ladders that was attached to wheels and ran along two walls of the store.

"He will say something like 'To tell you the truth, I don't think we have any more cornstarch.' Does that mean that at other times he is not telling the truth? English is very confusing sometimes."

There were boats in the bay now, men returning after a day's fishing. I watched the sea darkening and then lightening as the clouds passed over the sun. Odette was brushing the sand from her feet.

"I have to go," she said, reaching for her shoes.

Then I said something that I thought at the time was quite

inspired. Looking at her I said, "Don't put your shoes on right now."

"Why not?"

"Because," I said, "I like the way the water curls around your calves when you are walking in your bare feet through the waves." It never occurred to me that she might laugh at such a remark. The words had just come out, and I could see that she was regarding me in a slightly different way, a hint of a smile at the corners of her mouth. She reached over and gave me a little push.

"My legs and the water curling around them." She wanted to scoff perhaps, but she looked pleased as she gathered up the towel and her shoes and socks, the book of Tennyson's poems.

"I'll carry those," I said.

We had made our peace with each other, and Odette began to walk ahead through the water, sidestepping the waves, which were not high that day because of the offshore wind. But she laughed each time she avoided one, holding up her dress, vamping a little. A performance just for me! At the railway bridge the tracks were too hot to walk on and so we sat down to put on our shoes. She reached across and grabbed my hair.

"Look at you, Mister Strawhead. Your hair is so light. The sun has blanched it."

"Bleached," I said.

She shrugged. "Bleached, then." She paused. "Listen I have a question for you, James."

"What's that?"

"Why are you always in such a bad mood? I mean look at yourself. You are young, you are healthy. You've got two legs. You can run around and do what you like." She stopped.

I knew what she was doing; she was comparing me to Gabriel and I was coming up short.

"Think about it," she said. "You have all this and yet you act like you have all the cares of the world on your shoulders. You should spend more time at the hotel with your friend. He was looking for you yesterday."

"What makes you think he's my friend?" I said.

"Of course he's your friend. Gabriel likes you. He has no other friends."

"He has you," I said. I was hoping that she would clarify everything for me. Tell me just what kind of a friend she was. We were walking now across the bridge and looking down at the swiftly moving tidal water.

"Yes, maybe," she said, "but he needs a friend like you too. Another guy to talk to and be with."

I didn't like the sound of that. A friend like me meant not like her. Which meant that what went on between them was beyond friendship. All this time, I had been circling the entire subject: that closet in the hotel. Had she agreed to go in there with Gabriel?

"Gabriel," I said, "likes me only when I'm useful to him."

We had stopped to lean over the railing and look across at the marsh, which was draining as the tide ebbed. The gulls were poking their beaks into the shallow water.

"Useful?" said Odette. "What do you mean 'useful'?"

"Like when he wants me to stand guard over your little love nest."

I knew that expression from reading Aunt Margery's copies of *Flash,* a tabloid of the day that chronicled the shenanigans of prominent Toronto people who were often coyly implicated in headlines. *What Bay Street Bigshot Spends Weekends with Ladyfriend in Wasaga Beach Love Nest?* That sort of thing. Aunt Margery used to slide her copies under the cushions of the wicker chairs in the sunroom at the back of the house, but I had ferreted them out and become an avid consumer of these titillating speculations.

"What is this *love nest?*" Odette asked. "I don't know the word."

"The closet," I said. "In the corridor by the elevator."

When she heard this she laughed and then spat, a generous gob that we watched hit the water and quickly disappear seaward under the bridge.

"That?" she said. "That's what you call in English a love nest? Gabriel and his ideas. I told him it was crazy. Only he would think of such a thing. What if we got caught, I said. For sure, I would lose my job. He can be such a kid sometimes."

"That's true," I said.

"I told him he was nuts if he thought I was going to go in that closet with him."

"He told me," I said, "that Pauline would stay in the main hallway and my job was to stand guard by the elevator in case anyone used it."

She began to walk ahead along the tracks, balancing herself

on them, addressing the wind streaming through the uncut hay along the hillside.

"It was just one of his crazy ideas, James. You know Gabriel. He's a nice guy, but he's also full of shit."

That shopworn old phrase. Music to my ears.

The Saturday after my dinner with Gabriel was damp with a light but persistent rain, the sort of day visitors from North America often find provoking in England but that I've always liked, remembering a sabbatical year in London when I used to stand by my study window in our flat in Holland Park, looking out at people huddled under their black umbrellas at the nearby bus stop. From that window, I could also wave to my children in their slickers and plastic hats as they waited for their school van. After they were picked up, I went to my desk. To the notepads and books, the tidy pile of paper. I always felt secure and mildly elated indoors on such days, working on my manuscript, which then seemed so full of excitement and promise.

Almost a year free of teaching and committee responsibilities lay before me in that autumn of 1971. That year Susan was twelve, tall and self-assured for her age, entirely comfortable in the kilt and sweater of her new school, her dark hair cut short with bangs. Within weeks she had acquired traces of an English accent. Susan loved everything she encountered in England, the habits and customs of its people, its history, its Englishness. David was more wary of his new surroundings but adjusting all the same, a serious nine-year-old in knee stockings and grey short pants, the green shirt with its little gold crest. Both had made friends but were still regarded as rather exotic creatures by their English schoolmates. Except for my wife, we were a family of dedicated Anglophiles. Leah was stoic about it all, but she no longer felt at home in England. She didn't share my fondness for rainy days and my fussy insistence on tea and biscuits at four o'clock in the afternoon. She missed the bright, crisp days of the Canadian fall and the warmer houses. To her, England was old and grey and falling apart, a place she had left with her parents and brother after the war. Now she was back with me and the children and she would stick it out for a year, but she wouldn't pretend that she enjoyed it. Leah was then forty-three, a handsome dark-haired woman growing a little stout in her middle years, quiet and self-contained, an abiding melancholy accompanying her throughout life. She was much like her father, a medical doctor who also carried about him that abstracted air of sadness. No one could have foreseen then that Leah had only nine more years of life.

In my study in that Holland Park flat, I was trying to put together my great synthesis, rallying a century's aspirations and accomplishments around the banner of the Great Exhibition of 1851, with guest appearances by such luminaries as Darwin and Dickens, and, of course, Alfred Tennyson. In my elaborate pipe dream, I saw the telegraph and the onrushing steam engine, the smoke and noise of industrialism, the buzz of new ideas in the grimy Victorian air, the continuous hemorrhaging of religious faith; it was to be nothing less than the story of how we arrived at where we are today. That at least was the general idea. How many rainy days of that year did I sit at my desk dreaming of the final sentence that would bring it all to a resounding conclusion? And then the gracious acceptance letter from the publisher, the enthusiastic endorsements from experts in the field, the congratulations of colleagues who frankly hadn't thought I had it in me, the tasteful little launch party in one of the college's common rooms. I'm surely not alone in having embarked on a project beyond my powers to complete in any convincing way. Yet whenever I look at the boxed manuscript in my apartment in Toronto, I am sobered by the thought of the delusions that we harbour for so long.

I was thinking of all this as I shook the rain from my umbrella inside the doors of the Victoria and Albert Museum, where I intended to spend most of my day. I used to take Susan there on Saturdays during that sabbatical year. Together we inspected the moustache cups and snuff boxes, the brightly decorated biscuit tins and candlesticks. The sculpture of the black-and-white Newfoundland dog Bashaw, *The Faithful Friend of Man,* was still there on his mount of gilt bronze, stepping on the snake's neck, his eyes fixed on duties ahead. The great art critic, John Ruskin, scathingly dismissed this piece of Victorian kitsch, but my twelve-year-old daughter loved it and would stare at Bashaw in rapt admiration, as I suspect millions of others have done over the years. Susan was taking everything in, excited to be living in another country; it was something different, a year of her life that I hoped she would always remember. Standing in front of exhibits with her father, a young girl not far away from the complications of puberty, with one foot still in childhood but at ease in the presence of adults. Or have I imagined all that and was she just trying to please me?

That Saturday morning I was looking at something or other, a display case of Victorian pocket watches, I believe, when I had a little spell, an attack of nerves or anxiety, whatever you want to call it. At first I wondered about a heart attack, but no, this seemed more like knee-trembling panic. For a minute or so, I sat on a padded bench taking deep breaths and waiting for whatever it was to recede. But I knew I had to get out of the museum. Everything about the place was getting on my nerves—one of my mother's favourite expressions, when I think of it. So I did get out, making my way carefully (no use stumbling in haste) down the wide marble staircases to the lobby, thronged now with visitors, for it was nearly noon. Then out the door into the rain, unfurling my umbrella on the steps. I must have look flustered, an elderly man at odds with himself in some peculiar way, though no one seemed to take any notice. I set off at once along Cromwell Road, entered the first public house I could find, and ordered a large whisky. It did the job and I felt much better. Ordered a ham sandwich and a pot of tea and read a discarded copy of the *Daily Mirror*.

Half an hour later, I took a taxi to St. Paul's. I'm not sure now why I did that. Unless I felt that I might never again have the opportunity to see it. I know that in the taxi I was thinking of Gabriel staring gloomily out the darkened window of his limousine and of Susan in her big empty house at Woolford Abbey.

I wanted to phone her again, but I didn't know what to say. The evening before, we'd at least had my trip to Switzerland to talk about. But there was nothing more to be said about that. In front of St. Paul's I looked out at tourists taking pictures of themselves in front of Wren's great achievement and then told the driver to move on to my hotel. I felt indescribably tired and empty. I'm sure now that I had overextended myself; the old never learn and so eventually we have to submit to the notion that our bodies want to shut down for a while, perhaps for good. Taking off my jacket and shoes, I lay on the bed in my hotel room and was almost instantly asleep.

When I awakened, the long rectangle of light by the window had darkened. I heard the hiss of car tires on the wet street below and water dripping from eavestroughs. To my astonishment, it was five o'clock. I lay there for a few moments surveying my turned-out stockinged feet, the hands across my chest. It seems I hadn't stirred an inch during the hours I'd slept; I had lain there as composed and still as a corpse on display. This, I thought, is how I will look after the lights go out, unless I leave instructions to send my remains directly to the crematorium. I wondered then just whom to leave such information with—David probably. Then the phone rang, an unexpected and intrusive sound that in a hotel room can jar an aging heart. I fumbled with the receiver.

It was Adam calling to say that the limousine would pick me up the next morning between seven-thirty and eight o'clock, and so would I mind being ready by then. This news was oddly thrilling. Now that arrangements had been made and I was actually going to Zurich, it was as if I were now a part of something vaguely illicit, forbidden if not by law, at least by custom, by certain agreed-upon limits of contemporary social tolerance. It was like being invited to witness an execution, though of course that was nonsense. This was all being carried out at Gabriel's behest. He wanted to die, and certainly I had no moral compunctions about assisted suicide. If it came to that, I was inclined to approve for those who made the choice. Yet now that matters were in hand, I felt . . . *nonplussed* is the word, I suppose. I asked Adam about the sightseeing and how Gabriel had enjoyed his last day in London. Alas—and that was the very word this appealing young man used—the day had not been successful. After a couple of hours Gabriel had taken a bad turn. Adam blamed himself, a misjudgment with the medication for pain relief. In any case, Gabriel could not carry on, and so they had returned to the hotel. He was now heavily sedated and sleeping. I told Adam that I would be ready by seven-thirty the next morning and he thanked me again for accompanying them.

Without knowing what I wanted to say to her, I phoned Susan. I pictured her sitting alone in that enormous house looking out at the wet empty playing fields. Late Saturday afternoons are the loneliest hours of the week in boarding schools: the campus is quiet, the clamour of games long stilled; the day students have gone home and boarders too are often away for the weekend. I remember such afternoons at Groveland. Susan was a long time answering and when she did, seemed a little breathless, as if she had been running. As I had expected, she was surprised to hear from me again so soon. She told me she had been talking with one of the gardeners, who was spading a flower bed in front of the house. He was telling her about himself and his young family.

When she finished, all I could think to say was, "I just phoned to hear your voice, Sue."

She laughed. "Why, that's sweet, Dad, but are you all right? You sound a little funny."

"No, no, I'm quite all right." The last thing I wanted was to have her worrying about me. "I spent a little time in the V and A today," I said. "Remember how you and I used to go there on Saturday mornings? The year we lived over here? Do you remember the black-and-white dog, Bashaw?"

"Oh, Bashaw," she said, "of course I remember. Yes. How I loved him! He was killing a snake or something, wasn't he?"

"He still is," I said, and Susan laughed again.

"I always loved the V and A," she said. "I haven't been there in years. Roberta Penner in our history department organized a day trip for her senior class last February. I wanted to go along, but something came up. I can't remember what now."

Then she told me that she was going to the Vails' for dinner. Two or three other people she liked were coming along. Esther's husband, who apparently was a genius in the kitchen, was cooking. So there would be good food and wine and conversation. She was looking forward to it and I was glad that she was not going to be by herself on Saturday night, though I didn't say as much. I told her I was sorry I had interrupted her talk with the gardener and then said, "Maybe I'll call you from Switzerland."

"If you like," she said, "though it really isn't necessary, Dad. You're just going to be there for a few days, aren't you? I'm sure you and your old friend will have lots to talk about and things to see. Just enjoy yourself. Why not give me a call when you get home? I know you're worried, but things are as well as they can be for the moment. Believe it or not, the worst part was telling people and that's over now. Everyone here has been wonderful. I'm just taking things a day at a time. I know that's a tired old phrase, but like all clichés, it's the truth. It's about all you can do with this thing. Please don't fret about me, okay? Just enjoy your time with your friend and don't be too hard on poor little Switzerland and its cuckoo clocks."

We laughed at that, and I said, "Bless you, Sue." It didn't sound like me at all and Susan hesitated, as if to say something else.

Then she said, "Take care of yourself, Dad."

T hat summer I often pushed Gabriel's wheelchair along the main street of Percé to the wharf, where we watched the fishermen cleaning their day's catch, or looked out to sea through Gabriel's binoculars. On rainy days we stayed in his room listening to music and smoking. I was becoming more adept at inhaling the lethal fumes of those unfiltered Camels without gagging. Gabriel taught me how to play cribbage and we talked about our schools and what the world might be like when the war was over. He still clung to the hope that medical science might find a way to help him walk again. There was less bragging about his sex life, and in fact he surprised me one day by mentioning how the hallway closet had been a stupid idea. "It wouldn't have been fair to Odette," he said. It struck me that their relationship had evolved into something familiar and domestic.

The two girls finished work by three o'clock, but their ride back to our village wasn't until four, and so each afternoon Odette went to Gabriel's room for an hour, while Pauline and

I ostensibly stood guard in the hallway, though I don't know what we would have done had Mrs. F suddenly appeared. Gabriel, however, was confident that she would not be finished the bridge game before five, and this was true. And what, I wondered, would she discover if she had appeared? The truth is, I wasn't exactly sure what Gabriel and Odette were up to in his room. Were they just kissing and necking or was it the real thing? Gabriel would no longer say, and I found that both mystifying and reassuring. Perhaps he wasn't getting in after all. Such are the crumbs of hope nibbled upon by those left out of love's feast.

Pauline and I waited for them in the hallway near a window that overlooked the lawn and the tennis court. Pauline was a plump, amiable girl who seemed unsurprised by anything, greeting the vagaries of fortune with a good-natured shrug. Looking out at the tennis players, I practised my schoolboy French on her. "*Comment-allez vous aujourd'hui, mademoiselle? Je m'appelle Jacques. Il fait beau aujourd'hui, n'est-ce pas?*" She spoke only a little English and my feeble efforts in her language never failed to amuse her, for she would instantly redden and giggle, and sometimes give me a good push against the wall. It only occurred to me later that she was probably waiting to be kissed. Sometimes she would bring along Canadian comic books. They were in English and because of the war—some restrictions on the components of coloured ink, I suppose— they were in black and white. Pauline studied these avidly, her thick black eyebrows knitting in concentration as she examined the fantastical goings-on within the pages.

After a while the door would open and there would be

Gabriel, his hair a little messed, his face flushed. Odette too often had a high colour. Like a dutiful little housewife she always bent over and kissed him goodbye. I didn't like any of this, but I had adopted a sort of world-weary attitude, an acceptance that this was the way life sometimes unfolded.

One Saturday, my uncle dropped me off at the hotel. He told me it was Mrs. Fontaine's birthday and he wanted to visit the gift and souvenir shops. There was no sign of Gabriel or his mother on the veranda or in the lounge, and so I went up to Gabriel's room, the staff nodding to me as I climbed the stairs. By then I was a familiar sight, one of the American boy's entourage, another spoiled little *anglais* with money. I think I saw some of that in the faces of the bellhops and waiters in the St. Lawrence Hotel. Standing outside Gabriel's door, I could hear music and laughter, and when I knocked, the door was opened by Mrs. F, looking elegant in a smart red dress. She welcomed me with a hug, taking care not to spill her drink or burn me with her cigarette.

"James. You've come to help me celebrate. How delicious to see you."

Putting the cigarette in her mouth, she ruffled my hair and, linking arms, escorted me into the room, where I was surprised to see Odette sitting on the floor next to Gabriel's wheelchair. They were holding hands, Odette in a white blouse and skirt, her legs tucked demurely beneath her, a ribbon in her dark hair. She looked for all the world like a pretty young convent girl. Gabriel was in shirt and tie, blazer and slacks, a prep school boy on a date. So, I thought, it was now official. They were now boyfriend and girlfriend, with everything sanctioned by the mother who was smiling down at her darling boy and his little French-Canadian sweetheart.

Mrs. F was swaying to the phonograph music from Rodgers and Hammerstein's *Oklahoma!* "People Will Say We're in Love."

"Welcome, James," said Gabriel. "We're having a party for the old mater. Fifty-six today."

His mother gave a little shriek. "Gabriel Fontaine, I am going to wring your neck. Just see if I don't."

Gabriel made a wry face. "Well, okay. Maybe not fifty-six."

"Not even close, dear boy, and don't you say another word about it."

Odette was smiling. But how strange it all must have been to her. She had been admitted to the inner circle, was a friend now of wealthy guests, Cinderella at the ball. And I have to say that she didn't look in the least uncomfortable with any of it. Yet all afternoon I found myself worrying that something would spoil the day for her. That she would in some way be embarrassed or made to feel awkward. Looking back now I can see that Odette had far more savvy about how to fit in with the Fontaines than I thought.

My uncle came by later. He had been visiting the Porters in their room and both were unwell. Something they ate for lunch at a roadside diner. Uncle Chester had bought a present for Mrs. Fontaine, a necklace of seashells made by a local craftsman. Standing behind her like a suitor, he fastened it around her throat. She was delighted, and I marvelled at my uncle's knack for picking out something so perfectly suitable; mostly he lived his life apart from women, yet he knew precisely what might please them. They danced then, my uncle and Mrs. Fontaine, stepping lightly around the room to a wistful little waltz called "Out of My Dreams." Gabriel and Odette and I could not help applauding. Mrs. Fontaine said they were going out to dinner at a restaurant in the village.

"Just for a change from the dining room," she said. "It's Gabriel's present to me. He's invited me to dinner with him and his little friend and all I have to do is show up and pay for it. Which I thought was a charming idea—don't you, Chester?"

"Indeed I do," said my uncle, "perfectly charming."

"So you and James will join us of course. I'm sure they can find room for us all."

I didn't want to go. It was too painful for me to watch Odette looking at Gabriel the way she did, and I didn't think I could stand an entire evening of it. I was relieved when my uncle said we would unfortunately have to decline the invitation. Mrs. Moore was expecting us, and moreover was preparing one of her famous fish pies. We couldn't disappoint her. I have wondered from time to time whether Uncle Chester sensed that I was unhappy in the company of the lovers; that I had lost and wanted only to be alone to lick my wounds. So he would rescue me. It's possible. My uncle was an enigmatic man, hard to reach and probably more insightful about the human heart than he let on. Certainly that business about the fish pie was mendacious. There was no fish pie at Mrs. Moore's that evening, and neither of us ever saw the need to refer to his falsehood.

A couple of weeks later—it was August by then—we went on a picnic the four of us, Gabriel and Odette, Pauline and I. It was all arranged by Mrs. Fontaine, who seemed determined to make her son's summer holiday as normal as possible. And what could be more normal in summer than a picnic by the sea. This was on a Monday, the girls' day off, and under Mrs. Fontaine's instructions, the hotel provided a food hamper and bottles of Coca-Cola and Orange Crush fitted into a tub of ice. Before noon we met in front of the hotel, where an old Ford pickup truck awaited us, driven by a man named Emile. I recognized the truck as the one in which Odette rode to work each day. Emile also worked at the hotel, as a handyman. He was about forty, heavy-set and beetle-browed and with a surly manner. He spoke no English and so with gestures offered to lift Gabriel into the cab of the truck. Gabriel would have none of it, and insisted on making his own way up and into the passenger seat, an ordeal grimly endured and watched in silence by the rest of us. Emile then put the wheelchair, the food hamper, and the ice tub into the back, and the two girls and I climbed in and settled ourselves on blankets while Emile slammed the tailgate into place. On the steps of the hotel, the bellhops were watching, and I asked Odette if she wasn't bothered by the inevitable resentment of fellow workers. She only laughed.

"What do I care what they think? They're just jealous hicks. Isn't that the word you use in English for people who haven't been anywhere. Anyway, I'll soon be gone. As soon as my father gets a house for us in Montreal, I'll be gone. And in ten years I'll come back here and stay in that *maudit* hotel. And I'll bet you those same guys will still be there to carry the bags up to my room."

We felt extravagantly happy, animated by the novelty of

riding backward in the open air, the wind rushing at us from all directions, flattening our hair and at times taking our breath away. Now and then Gabriel would tap at the rear window and grin at us, and Odette would brush the hair from her eyes and stick out her tongue at him. The gravel road was rough and with every lurch and bump, the girls would swear in French. I recognized the words because on one of our Monday walks, Odette had taught me how most French profanity came from the language of the Church.

"That tells you something about the Catholic religion, doesn't it?" she had said.

She was smoking a cigarette, puffing away angrily, in a terrible mood after quarrelling with her mother that morning.

"What does it tell me?" I asked.

"Never mind," she said, "never mind."

But on the day of the picnic, the girls' cursing at the bumpy road was good-natured. We were all happy, and looking up at the clouds sailing across the blue sky, I thought of the strangeness of the entire experience; there I was in the back of a truck in the wilds of Quebec with two girls I hadn't known existed only six weeks before.

A few miles from Percé, we turned off the highway and drove down a road that fell steeply towards a cove. Emile stopped a few hundred feet from the water and we climbed out. While Emile busied himself with Gabriel's chair, I carried the food hamper across a field to an old wild apple tree. It looked like a perfect place to enjoy lunch out of the sun. Odette and Pauline followed, each grasping a handle of the washtub with its ice and pop. Meantime Gabriel had got himself out of the truck and was sitting in the wheelchair by the side of the road. The girls and I went back to him, and we all watched Emile drive farther down the road to a place where he could turn around. From there he gunned the truck up the hill, passing us without a glance as we stood in the dust. He seemed to be out of sorts, perhaps doing an errand he didn't like, or maybe it was his normal disposition. We watched the truck climb the hill, then turn onto the highway and disappear. Pauline told us he would be back at three o'clock. She said this in French and Odette translated. Pauline was the only one Emile had said a word to.

It was hot when the clouds gave way to sunlight, and getting Gabriel's wheelchair across that field was a struggle. The ground was rutted and uneven, dotted everywhere with old cow pats and hoof marks in the long grass. It was no place for a wheelchair, but we managed, Gabriel urging us on with his tomfoolery.

"Keep at it, troops. An oasis ahead. There's a cigarette and a drink for all at the end of the road."

And it really was a little oasis there under the tree among the speckled windfalls with the leafy branches overhead. We spread the blankets and smoked while Gabriel mixed rum and Cokes. The girls were excited to be there, though Odette continued to gripe about Emile.

"That son of a gun should have carried everything over here," she said. "That's what he's paid for."

"Forget it, kiddo," said Gabriel, "we're having a picnic, so drink up and enjoy. Why don't you all go for a swim before we eat?"

I liked the idea because I wanted to show off. I was not a

particularly good swimmer, but my Australian crawl was passable, and at least it was something I could do that Gabriel couldn't. That was really all that mattered.

The girls walked behind some trees to change, Gabriel following their progress through his binoculars, calling out, "Be careful that you don't get bitten in your precious little parts." He was in high spirits, already a little drunk, sipping his rum and Coke while I changed into my trunks. He told me he was anxious to see Odette in her new bathing suit. He'd bought it for her at one of the shops in Percé. At least he had paid for it; Odette herself had picked it out. I don't know why this bothered me, but it did. I couldn't have said so at the time, but I probably felt that giving a girl something like that was either too intimate or too patronizing. Maybe both. Still, Odette had a new bathing suit.

We watched them return, carrying their clothes against their chests, stepping carefully through the grass. Odette's bathing suit was a dark blue two-piece that showed her pale midriff and her wonderful legs. Pauline, however, had only a fussy looking old-fashioned costume tricked out by a little skirt. It had once been red but was now a faded pink, a hand-me-down from an older sister perhaps. It looked faintly comic on her chubby white body, though it didn't seem to bother her. Both were wearing those rubber bathing caps that made their faces look pinched and oddly unfamiliar until you got used to them. For a moment the three of us stood under the tree, shivering in the breeze and looking a bit anemic beside Gabriel with his lean brown arms and face. He had put on his aviator's glasses, and I had to admit the bastard looked like a movie star sitting there.

"Well, what are you waiting for, gang?" he said. "Away you go."

"Come on, James," said Odette, taking my hand, "we'll go in together."

My head was buzzing from the rum and Coke, but nothing was going to stop me from holding the hands of those two girls and running down that road to the sea. They were shriek-ing with delight as we hit the water. The Gulf of St. Lawrence is always cold, even in August, but I was still shocked by those tons of freezing water around and over me. Still, I quickly left the girls behind, swimming underwater for as long as I could, surfacing finally to discover that I was a long way out, the swell of the sea partly obscuring the land. As I started back, I hoped Odette would be worried about me, but she and Pauline were too busy laughing and splashing each other. Dog-paddling was about all they could manage and they were keeping close to shore. Farther away I could see Gabriel, a distant figure in his chair under the tree.

When I reached the girls, they tried at once to put me under, the two of them grasping my arms, leaning on my shoulders and head. The sudden closeness of them was rapturous to a boy who had never before touched a girl, and as I soon discovered, a certain licence had been unwittingly granted in the circum-stances; we were now free to disport ourselves erotically with hands on arms and backs and stomachs, fingers brushing thighs and breasts, and now and then my helpless erection, which I felt would surely erupt at any moment. *Delectable.* It was all *delectable*, the more so for my knowing that Gabriel could only watch this horseplay through his expensive binoculars. Mean-spirited? Without a doubt, but I could no more help it than I could help swimming under Odette and clasping her thighs, drawing her downward and in so doing, pass a glancing hand across her breasts. Surfacing she would spit a mouthful of water at me and laugh.

When we came ashore to dry off, Gabriel was applauding and shouting, "Bravo, bravo, come forth, you nymphs and satyr, it's time to eat."

Odette had taken off her bathing cap and was shaking her hair back into place. "What's he talking about?"

"Nothing," I said. "I think he's hungry."

She was looking up towards Gabriel, squinting in the sunlight, and watching her I wondered if she was nearsighted and needed glasses.

"We'd better feed him, then," she said. "Before he gets too drunk."

I hadn't noticed her squinting before, and it left me with a feeling of almost unbearable tenderness. If Odette needed glasses, I would get them somehow. I resolved to ask her when we were on one of our walks, though in fact I never did. By the time we reached Gabriel, our bathing suits were cold and damp and the girls went off again to change. Odette was right about Gabriel. He was getting lit up with all that rum and Coke, though he was usually quite good at hiding it. Maybe that was why his mother never suspected that he drank as much as he did, but I may be exaggerating just how much he really did drink. The truth is, I don't really know. Some of it could have been an act. I had learned, however, that a sure sign that he was on his way was his cruel tongue.

"That little fat girl of yours," he said, "she's got quite the set of knockers on her."

"She's not exactly my girl," I said.

"Have you had your hands on them yet?"

"Maybe."

"After we eat, why don't you take her for a little walk? I think Odette and I would like to be alone."

"I can take a hint, Gabriel."

"There could be something in it for you, pal. I've watched that girl looking at you."

The hotel had provided everything from tablecloth to plates and cutlery. There were cold chicken sandwiches, pickles and relish, jam tarts, a small apple pie, even linen napkins. An Edwardian picnic lunch there under the apple tree. After we'd finished eating and the girls had cleared things away, Gabriel said, "The Lone Ranger will soon be back, don't you think? What time did he say, Odette?"

"Three o'clock," she said.

Gabriel looked at his watch and tapped it. "We have an hour and a half, troops."

This I took as my cue to ask Pauline if she wanted to go for a walk along the beach. Odette said something to her in French, and Pauline giggled and got to her feet.

As we left, Odette called out, "Don't do anything I wouldn't do."

"And what would that be?" I called back, but she only laughed. She was already helping Gabriel from his chair. He was leaning on her and then they seemed to sink together onto the blanket. Apparently she was the only one allowed to lay hands on him.

As for Pauline and me, we must have been an odd sight had anyone been on the beach to see us, I with my unruly straw-coloured hair, tall and skinny, and Pauline, dark-haired and something of a roly-poly figure—she came up only to my chest. We walked along in silence. That air of playfully innocent sexuality we'd enjoyed in the water had long evaporated, and now we had to find other ways into an intimacy that I wasn't sure either of us really wanted. I knew we had to talk about something. We needed words. But even if we had known each other's language, what would we talk about? With Odette it was easy. At times you couldn't shut her up. She was curious and opinionated. I could have a conversation with Odette on almost anything. But Pauline and I were locked into wordless-ness, timid and shy.

The day was clouding over, the sun emerging only now and then to spear us with a shaft of hot light. After ten minutes, we came upon an enormous rock jutting ten feet into the sea, effectively blocking our way. But next to it, sheltered from the wind, was a patch of dry sand with a weathered log and ashes from an old fire. We lay down together without a word, resting our heads against the log. Pauline closed her eyes while I lay thinking of Odette and Gabriel. What would they be talking about? Or would they be in such a state of frenzy that words were superfluous? But no. I knew that both would use words in their lovemaking. They would use words perfectly and natu-rally. Then I wondered what Pauline was thinking, lying there in the sand beside me. I was certain that she saw me as a hopeless case. In those days the word used by girls to dismiss boys like me was *drip*. I was a *drip*, and I wondered if there was a similar term in French. Most likely, I decided, there was a word for people like me in every language. I thought about this as I studied Pauline's face in repose. Was she thinking about the day itself? I wondered. A day that was like no other in her life; a Monday in which she ate sandwiches and tarts made by her fellow workers at the hotel. And all this in the company of rich boys. She even drank rum with them. A day in her life she might always remember. But then, maybe she wasn't thinking that way at all. Maybe she just took things as they came. You never can tell what will happen to you from one day to the next, and so what? Let it happen. Things will probably turn out all right. I don't even know now if I thought all that about Pauline Legault, but I probably did, for that was the kind of boy I was. What I do know is that at one point I leaned over and, closing my eyes, pressed my lips against her small pretty mouth, a little rosebud. She may have been half asleep, for she moved her head away as if resisting and then opened her eyes to look at me.

"No, no," she said. "Like this." And then she kissed me and I felt her tongue in my mouth.

There followed some prolonged wrestling there on the sand, an hour of long kisses in which, eyes closed tight, we nearly choked on each other's tongues. In her good-natured way Pauline allowed me certain liberties with her stout little body. I was permitted, for example, to touch her breasts, but she would not allow my hands under her sweater. At first I squeezed away, as if inspecting exotic fruit, and for this she slapped my hand.

"*Doucement*," she cried, "*doucement.*"

These were the fumbling rituals of courtship in an age when a boy was mostly on his own, unaided by graphic film or porn site on the Internet. It was all clumsy and rather sweet, and when Pauline and I walked back, we were holding hands, paired off at last as boy and girlfriend. According to the unwritten laws of love, I'd got second prize—and perhaps it was all I deserved.

As we walked up the road towards the tree in the field, I could see that Odette and Gabriel were not clinging half-naked to each other as I'd feared. He was back in his wheelchair, smoking and watching our approach, with Odette sitting at his feet and leaning against him, a picture of contentment and youthful beauty. The end to a perfect summer afternoon, you might think, but, no, things soon fell asunder.

It began with the changing weather, a grey wall of rain darkening the water as it crossed towards us. It was now past three o'clock and the Ford truck was nowhere to be seen. At first the rain was gentle enough, but soon it was beating hard upon the field and we huddled under the branches and dripping leaves, Odette cursing Emile in two languages. For twenty minutes, perhaps a half-hour, we waited, bedraggled and increasingly glum, before we saw the truck turning off the highway, its headlights on, the windshield wipers going madly as it splashed through puddles on the road down to the bottom of the hill to turn around.

Odette was scornful. "The stupid bastard will get stuck. It's all boggy down there now."

And he nearly did, the tires whining in the mud, blue smoke pouring from the tailpipe as he rocked the truck back and forth between first gear and reverse, freeing it finally and returning up the hill, where he stopped and waited for us. Clearly he had no intention of getting out into the rain before he had to. Odette called him an arsehole.

She and Pauline then ran across the field with the picnic gear and dumped it into the back of the truck, while I began to push Gabriel's chair. It didn't take long to see that it was going to be difficult. The rain had now soaked the ground, and soon the wheels sank into the rough, soft earth and stopped. Even with the girls pulling and my pushing, we could move the wheelchair only inches at a time. It was exhausting, discouraging work, and Gabriel, trying perhaps to bear up to the indignity of it all, looked on impassively as he was tugged this way and that, hating, I imagined, every minute of his terrible dependence on others. I thought of carrying him. But would he let me? And could I manage it? Perhaps the three of us could try something called a fireman's chair, a manoeuvre I had seen demonstrated at Cadet inspection, whereby two or three boys carried a supposedly injured fellow to safety. But I wasn't sure how it worked, and besides, we needed his permission.

"Can we carry you to the truck, Gabriel?" I asked.

"No," he replied, summoning a final attempt at encouragement. "We'll make it, comrades. Just keep at it. Shoulder to the wheel and all that." But his patience was waning and he looked grim. Very grim.

The three of us bent again to the task, and the wheelchair rocked forward a few inches and stopped. Breathing hard, Odette straightened up.

"*Tabernac,*" she muttered, "it's stuck. It can't be done like this."

She looked fed up and, to me, beautiful, even with her hair plastered to her skull. Her blouse was soaked through and I could see her brassiere. Pauline had sat down to catch her breath. Odette looked back at the truck.

"That good-for-nothing is going to have to get off his arse and help out here."

"No," said Gabriel, "you can do it."

"No, Gabriel," she said. "We can't."

And with that she turned and walked quickly across the field. We watched as she stood by the truck, shouting and waving her arms and pointing back towards us. After a while Emile got out. He settled a flat tweed cap on his head, buttoned his jacket, and followed her, a stolid figure moving through the rain, getting his own soaking at last. And he did not look pleased when he arrived.

Odette was speaking to him in French, explaining, I gathered, that we had to push the wheelchair across the field because Gabriel did not like being carried. Under the cap the man's broad face was creased in a frown. He was obviously trying to make sense out of what she was saying. The solution must have appeared simple to him. Carry the boy to the truck. Come back for the wheelchair. Drive to the hotel. I was guessing that this was going through his mind, but nevertheless, Odette persuaded him to try her way. So now the four of us began pulling and pushing, at one point nearly upsetting the chair.

Emile was panting, his face darkened with exertion and anger. You could tell he'd had enough of four kids in a wet field, and who could blame him? We were getting nowhere. Still, what happened next was alarming and it happened so quickly that everyone was taken by surprise, including Gabriel. Without a word Emile bent down and, lifting Gabriel from the chair, began to carry him across the field towards the truck. Then the screaming started, a torrent of cursing such as I had never heard in my life and hope never to hear again. All we could do was follow them in the rain and listen to it, looking at Emile's broad back with Gabriel howling in his arms.

Children have tantrums and they can often be painful to witness. But a sixteen-year-old boy is nearly an adult, and Gabriel's performance that afternoon was profoundly embarrassing; it was disproportionate, outrageous, an insult to reason. It made you want to hide from humanity for a week, and think only about primordial mineral life, about layers of lava flowing and hardening over millions of years. When we reached the truck, Gabriel was sitting on the running board, where Emile had left him before getting in himself and slamming the door. The three of us busied ourselves lifting the heavy chair into the back of the truck. Gabriel's only words to us were hoarsely whispered.

"Give me my sticks."

Odette handed him the two canes, and leaning on them, he stood up and slowly turned around to open the door. Then began his agonizingly slow ascent as he threw up his sticks and crawled into the cab and onto the seat.

After he closed the door, I secured the tailgate and the girls and I climbed into the back under the damp blankets, grateful to be away from that helpless rage. I don't think we said a word to one other as we were jolted onward to the highway and back to Percé.

In Zurich we stayed at the elegant Baur au Lac on Talstrasse, in the heart of town, overlooking the lake. When we'd arrived early Sunday afternoon, Gabriel had elicited a raised eyebrow or two from the rather staid clientele in the lobby by saying, "I seem to have spent a good part of my life checking in and out of these fucking places. This will be the last one, so hallelujah." In his overcoat and muffler he looked haggard, but for a man who would be dead within twenty-four hours, he was in remarkable spirits, excited as a child on holidays. On the flight from London he had joked with the cabin attendant, a lovely young woman.

"We'll have some champagne," he had said. "I and my young travelling companion here—and that sober-looking gent," he added, pointing to me across the aisle. "We have to cheer him up."

She gave me an appraising smile. "I'll do my best, sir."

"I know you will, my dear, I know you will," said Gabriel.

Adam smiled but looked mildly concerned, perhaps wondering if the champagne would upset Gabriel's ravaged innards and if he would soon have a mess on his hands. But it all went well. Gabriel had only the one glass, and Adam and I two each. In the nearly empty first-class cabin, my eye was sometimes on another traveller as we crossed the English Channel, a striking young woman, her face partly hidden behind enormous sunglasses. She sat alone, a few aisles away, staring out the window, looking glamorous and stricken. I imagined the end of a love affair, seeing or perhaps wanting to see in everyone a sadness at the heart of life.

When we landed, Adam navigated the wheelchair through the airport. How light and compact wheelchairs are nowadays compared to that cumbersome, old wooden thing I had pushed through the streets of Percé over sixty years ago. In the parking area the driver of the minibus was waiting. Throughout it all Gabriel was a model of forbearance, complaining only once of being cold, though it was a sunny day and warm for the season. On the way into the city, Adam asked the driver to turn up the heat. Gabriel told me he was going to have a rest and then we would have a look around.

"The Old Town is supposed to be interesting," he said. "I didn't take the trouble to look the last time we were here. We were just in and out—right, Adam?"

"That's right, sir."

"In and out," laughed Gabriel. "I suppose you could say the same thing this time. I'm in and then I'm out. But this time I'll really be out." The phrase seemed to delight him and he laughed again. "Anyway, James, we'll see what it's like. Some famous people have spent time here. Lenin lived in Zurich, and that crazy artist—what was his name, Adam?"

"Salvador Dalí, sir."

"Yes, Dalí. He did that picture with the clock melting over the table. And the Irish writer Joyce. He's buried here, I believe. Anyway, we'll have a look around. We'll meet you in the lobby at four."

So I went to my room and read a few pages of a new biography of William Gladstone, looking out the window from time to time at a little park in front of the hotel. Through the trees I could see the colourful blue trolleys on the Gurson Quai and beyond that the lake with its Sunday afternoon sailboats. In the distance the snow on the Alps. Picturesque in its own way, but I was restless, still baffled by the strange turnings my life had taken in the nine days since Susan had called me. I kept thinking that I should have been on a flight to Toronto, trying to ignore the corny movie by reading this biography, a book I knew I would never finish and in fact would leave behind in that hotel. The book was too big, too overburdened with detail. Reading it over the past week at three o'clock in the morning in a vain attempt to induce sleep had only left me impatient and irritable. Wide awake I had wanted to hurl it across the room. Nearly a thousand pages to tell the story of a man's life. Just another kind of howling. I had put it into my carry-on bag at the last minute and lugged it around airports and hotel lobbies. But finally on that Sunday afternoon in Zurich I'd had enough, so I shoved the great, fat thing onto a ledge in a corner of the closet, hoping it wouldn't be discovered until I'd left. The

Swiss are so efficient and dutiful that I had visions of the head
of housekeeping approaching me as I checked out and pressing the tome upon me. "You forgot this, sir." But as I was hiding
it in the closet, I felt that I was doing something distinctly odd,
something my poor mother might have done at some point
in her life.

So I was not on a flight to Toronto, but standing by a window in an expensive hotel in Switzerland, a country I had
never imagined visiting, a country once famous for its watch-
making skills. The first book I remember reading on my own,
the story of Heidi living with her grandfather on the slopes
and meadows of the mountains, was set in Switzerland. Now
it was a place for the rich to ski and store money. Or come to
die. I was feeling as beset and unsettled as I had been the day
before at the Victoria and Albert Museum. Apparently another
frontal assault on my nerves was underway, and I knew I had
to get out of that room. A walk, then, to calm down.

The streets were filled with tourists, mostly French or
German. The cafés and coffee houses on Bahnhofstrasse were
open to the summery weather, and I was surrounded by healthy-
looking, prosperous people enjoying themselves. I walked down
to the Limatt and watched a tourist boat gliding by, the passengers taking pictures of the city. Happy, happy people briefly
removed from their worries by the novelty of it all. It's hard to
be unhappy on a boat on a sunny afternoon. But when all was
said and done, I could not escape that easily. Even there, perhaps especially there among the tourists and burghers of that
rich little city, I had to confront the facts: I was there to be with
a man who had decided he was finished with all this. And my

daughter would soon face a day when she too might tire of the well-being of those around her, tire of others with their health and their store of unregarded days.

I was thinking of all this as I walked by the river, and I must have worked myself into a state, for I felt suddenly that I might be having a seizure, a stroke perhaps or heart attack. No particular pain, but my entire system seemed overwhelmed, and I must have staggered a bit. Fortunately there was an empty bench nearby, and I lurched towards it and sat there panting and sweating. A disquieting moment, though I felt ashamed of myself, for there was no dizziness or pressure in my arms or chest. It was just nerves, and we are always ashamed of our nerves. But my pale face and stagger had been noticed. A young man and a woman—university students, by the look of them—had been walking along the path towards me, and now the young woman hurried over to the bench. She was nineteen or twenty and very pretty, with blond curly hair and blue eyes. Heidi, grown up at last and in tank top and jeans. The word *winsome* came to mind as she sat down beside me and placed a hand on my arm. Her boyfriend, dark-haired with a five o'clock shadow (when did young men stop shaving?), stood apart from us. The woman said something to me in German. Her breath was faintly sweet as if she'd been eating chocolate.

"I'm afraid I don't speak German," I said. My old thudding heart was slowing down.

"That's all right," she said, "I speak some English. Are you okay? You looked like you had a sickness. The way you walked to the bench."

"Yes, I thought so too," I said, "but I'm feeling better now that I'm sitting down."

She hadn't let go of my arm and I didn't want her to; it was reassuring, that young woman's hand on my arm. It is women who will see to us in the end, I thought. They will rub our aching backs and hold our hands. The girl then looked up and said something to the man in German. It sounded harsh, a little bossy, but then German often sounds like that, doesn't it. The young man shrugged. What a dolt! And she was with him. Who can explain these things?

"I have a phone," she said. "Would you like the ambulance?"

"No, no," I said. "I think I'm all right now. It was anxiety perhaps."

I don't know if she understood the word, but she was looking directly at me with those blue eyes. Such clear eyes in the young. So full of health. Her skin. Her hair. How I longed to unburden myself to this young woman. To sit on that bench with her warm hand on my arm, and tell her about my daughter and Gabriel and my absolute loneliness in a foreign city. At the same time I was aware of being just a foolish, foolish old man.

Heidi had taken off her backpack and opened up a bottle of water. "Take some," she said.

She was a bossy little creature, after all, and I did as I was told, drinking gratefully.

"Are you sure about the ambulance?" she asked.

"Yes, I'm sure," I said. "You've been very kind. I'm just overtired. I'll rest a little and then go back to my hotel."

She smiled. "That's good. You will be okay now?"

"Yes. Perfectly fine. I can't thank you enough for your kindness."

"No problem," she said, patting my arm again, bless her, and getting up.

I watched them walk away. She had linked her arm in his, and she looked back once more to wave at me before they disappeared behind others on the path. Leaning back I closed my eyes for a moment, feeling the sun on my face. I needed to talk to someone who knew me. To a member of my family. Or to Catherine Parmeter. I had thought I had got used to life without her company, but at moments like that we remember how it was to have someone in whom to confide. What time was it in Auckland, anyway? What might she be doing at that moment?

It was almost four o'clock when I returned to the hotel. In the lobby I recognized an American film star, a middle-aged man whose name I could not recall but whose face was familiar. I seldom go to movies any more, but such is the osmotic effectiveness of popular culture that you can't help recognizing Hollywood faces. And on the man's arm was the young woman from our flight that morning, still wearing the large shades and laughing at something said by her famous consort. So much for her looking "stricken" and my theory of a failed affair.

In my room the little red light on the phone was pulsing and I listened to Adam's voice recorded at 3:42. Gabriel was not at his best, and so the jaunt around Old Town was off. Could I come to their suite for cocktails at five? Food would also be provided. Gabriel had announced that he was finished with hotel dining rooms. It would likely be an early night for him, Adam said.

During that summer in the Gaspé, my father sent me things just as he had when I was at Groveland School. A chemistry set. A baseball mitt. A book of famous sea battles recounting the exploits of men like Drake and Nelson. Their selection always struck me as an afterthought on his part. As if, hurrying through an Ottawa department store in search of a necktie for himself or perfume for his girlfriend, he happened to recall that he had a son and should perhaps send him something—for isn't that what fathers did from time to time? These gifts were never accompanied by any note of greeting or inquiry as to how I was faring. Just a box in brown mailing paper with something in it. That August he sent me a kit for a model airplane, a Lancaster bomber. I can still see the picture on the box, the dull green fuselage with its big, red bull's eye. I pictured J. T. noticing a stack of these boxes on a store counter and thinking, *Now here's something a boy would like.* It would never have occurred to him that I had neither the patience nor the aptitude to glue and assemble the bits and pieces of balsa wood and paper into something resembling an airplane. Besides, I was then, in my own mind at least, a couple of years too old for such pastimes.

The box of airplane parts arrived during the week of our picnic. I was still furious over Gabriel's childish display that afternoon, and had once again refused to go to Percé with my uncle. This he found aggravating, for he could see no reason behind my refusal and I wasn't about to tell him. He put it all down to my habitual moodiness, which was partly true. So again we had stopped speaking and were avoiding each other whenever possible. Nor had I spoken a word to Odette during that week. I saw her only from my attic window as she went to work each morning and returned in the afternoon. I was sulking like Achilles in his tent, no question about it. As childish in my own way as Gabriel had been in his. And how I missed talking to her. I knew she would have forgiven him for his tantrum and I wanted to argue with her about that. Convince her that he was nothing more than a spoiled brat—and why should he always have his own way? I knew, however, that the longer I left things as they were, the harder it would be to approach her. That left me thinking that the model airplane kit might be useful. If I were to give it to one of her brothers while she was at work, perhaps she would see that despite my spells of reclusive grumpiness, I was not such a bad fellow. The oldest boy, Maurice, was about thirteen and he seemed the most likely candidate for the gift. But what was the word for "gift" in French? I had taken French at Groveland, but I hadn't paid much attention and barely passed. The teacher wasn't very good and none of us could really see the point of learning it.

One morning I walked across the field between our houses. A farmer rented the surrounding land for its hay, and all week he had been working at it. I used to watch him as he sat on the iron seat of his mower behind a dapple grey horse. After he was finished mowing, he returned with a many-pronged apparatus that raked the hay into long windrows. A few days later his sons used pitchforks to stack it into haycocks, and it was among these that I walked on my way to the Huards' house with my box of airplane parts. The black-and-white collie soon got wind of me and charged forth barking; from time to time I could see his long, snouted face and white tail among the haycocks as he ran towards me. On the Huards' gallery, one of the children yelled at him. But I was not afraid of the dog, for I knew he was harmless, and when he reached me, he merely bounded about, sniffing my trouser legs and shoes. Odette's brothers and sisters had stopped playing and now stood watching me. What was the young *anglais* up to now? He was Odette's friend and he must know that she was away at work. And what was he carrying? When Odette and I went on our walks, we always met at the gate of their laneway, and so this was the first time I had seen the Huards up close. I was struck by how poor they were in their patched and cast-off clothes. I had seen kids like them on the streets of the little town near our school. They had watched us Groveland boys on our way to a Saturday matinee at the Roxy Theatre with the same guarded eyes that I saw in the Huards, a look of sullen deference to authority in whatever guise—the priest, the store manager, the young English-speaking stranger. Behind the screened front door, I could just make out the figure of

Odette's mother standing with her arms folded across her chest. Her oldest son, Maurice, sat on the front steps of the gallery. Almost my age but smaller, a dark-haired, unfriendly-looking boy. Years later, in the early sixties, I read in one of the Toronto papers about a bank robbery in Montreal in which a bystander was killed in a gunfight between the police and the thieves who were captured. Their mug shots were in the paper, and in one of them I saw the same wary eyes in a thirty-year-old Maurice Huard.

On that August morning in 1944, however, Maurice was only thirteen when I handed him the airplane kit. Oddly enough, as I did so, the French word for "gift" came to mind. *Un cadeau.* I must have mumbled it, but he still looked puzzled, and who could blame him? What was this all about? The others remained silent. Even the dog had stopped barking and lay in the yard looking up at me, his long tongue hanging out as he panted. I knew I was handling everything badly, but I felt shy and misplaced among all those staring faces. Turning quickly I left without a word, walking as fast as I could back across the field. The whole clumsy venture left me feeling humiliated and angry with myself. In my attic room, I sat down at once and wrote a letter to my mother, exaggerating the circumstances of my exile, emphasizing my loneliness, mocking Uncle Chester's manner and habits, the Porters' Boston accent, the sight of Mrs. Moore's backside as she bent across her vegetable garden in the mornings. It was a mean-spirited little missive but writing it was purgative and thoroughly enjoyable. I didn't mention the model airplane. Whether that letter gave my already burdened mother guilty misgivings about my ban-

ishment, or whether it merely provoked laughter at my outrageous caricatures, I'll never know.

That evening after supper I heard my uncle calling up the
stairs to me, and when I went down, I happened to glance out
the front window and there was Odette, sitting on the veranda
steps. Like a child she was aiming the model plane as if tempted
to throw it into the air. I could hear the clatter of dishes from
the kitchen, but my uncle was still at the dining room table
finishing his tea and looking out at the sunset, jotting observations into his notebook. The author at work. I was testy.

"You could at least have shown her in," I said.

This bit of cheek was met with a thin smile; moreover, it
brought Mrs. Moore into the dining room, where she stood
glowering at me while she polished a plate with her tea towel.
Mrs. Moore fancied herself up on manners and she looked far
from pleased.

"Oh, but we did, dear boy," said Uncle Chester. "Did we not,
Mrs. Moore?"

"We most certainly did," said Mrs. Moore.

I think she could have throttled me there and then. My
uncle was again staring at the sky behind the dark hills.

"The young lady preferred not to come in," he said.

When I opened the front door, Odette looked up.

"Here's your plane," she said.

"I don't want it," I said. "I gave it to him. It was a gift."

"Maurice thought you wanted him to put it together for you.
So he did. A pretty good job too, I think."

"But I told him it was a gift. I said *un cadeau*. Isn't that French
for 'gift'?"

She shrugged. "Yes, but maybe he didn't hear you. He's a little deaf in one ear." She shrugged again. "Or he might have wondered why you would be giving him a gift. *I* am wondering why you would give him a gift. So is everybody else in the house."

She got up and brushed her skirt. It was too complicated to explain, and anyway I felt tongue-tied. Foolish.

"Never mind," Odette said. "I will take it back to him. Maurice is very . . . what do you call it in English? *Timide?* Around most people he hangs back."

"Shy?"

"Shy," she said, repeating the word several times as if amused by its short, bright sound. "What a funny little word! *Shy.* Yes, that's what he is."

She began walking towards the house and I caught up to her.

"Look, Odette, I'm sorry about all this."

"Don't be sorry, James," she said. "It's a nice present." She laughed. "And all the time Maurice thought you just wanted him to put it together for you. What a donkey he is."

"But I would never ask him to do something like that."

"How does he know?"

"He doesn't, I guess."

"There you are, then."

We were walking through the hayfield towards her house. With the sun down the air was already cool. There were lights now in village houses. In another field, a cow was bawling for her calf, which must have strayed. Suddenly Odette was running ahead of me holding the model plane aloft, shouting as she ran. Maurice Huard, his hands deep in his pockets, was standing on the gallery watching his sister. Odette then threw the little airplane and we watched it soar briefly through the darkening air and fall to the ground. When I caught up to her, Odette was bent over, breathing hard and laughing.

"I smoke too much, I think," she said. "I can't run any more."

Maurice had jumped down from the gallery and run over to get the airplane.

"What were you saying to your brother?" I asked.

"I said the airplane was a gift from you. I also told him he was a donkey. Come on, let's go for a walk before it gets too dark. Let's go up in the field. Now that they've cut the hay."

We walked up the sloping field towards the brow of the hill, where cattle were grazing on the other side of the fence. From there we could see down to the houses in the village with their lighted windows, and the road and the bay. There was little traffic on the road. Few people in the village had a car, and the tourists were now in their cabins and motor courts. Odette and I stood by the fence looking down at it all. Behind us the heavy dark shapes of animals were moving; you could hear them cropping the grass and shitting. Odette and I seemed awkward with each other.

Finally she said, "Gabriel wonders why you have been away all week. He misses you."

"I'm browned off with him," I said. "All that stuff at the picnic. When the guy picked him up. Gabriel was crazy acting the way he did. Nuts. A little kid wouldn't have carried on like he did."

Odette spoke very softly.

"Gabriel doesn't like to be touched. You know that, James. And that son-of-a-whore Emile didn't even ask. He just picked up Gabriel like he was a bag of potatoes or something. And carried him off. It was a stupid thing to do. Gabriel is proud. You know that."

"So we all stand around in the rain because he's proud."

"We'd have got him out in his wheelchair, the four of us. With a little more time and patience we could have done it. With someone like Gabriel, you have to be patient. The boy is crippled. He'll never walk again. Just imagine that! He'll never do what we're doing right now. Walking up in this field and looking out at all this as if it's nothing. We can do this every day. Just think about him in that wheelchair. He's proud and he's hurt because you haven't been around to see him all week. You're supposed to be his friend."

I'd heard all this before.

"Gabriel," I said, "is a pain in the ass. A spoiled rich brat."

"You always say that, don't you. And you? What are you? A fucking sorehead. Yes, that's what you are. Young Mister Sorehead who spends all day up in his room playing with himself, I bet."

I walked away from her then, striding down the hill. I imagine I was close to tears. After a while I heard her behind me running to catch up. Grabbing me by the arm.

"I'm sorry I said that. It was stupid. I can be stupid. Stop and listen to me now."

She had pulled me to a halt and we stood there looking at each other.

"I like you, James, and I want to be your friend. Don't be sore at me, okay? I'm sorry I said that."

I felt the grip of her hand on my arm, smelt her faintly sour breath. I was mortified by everything, choked up with humiliation and the rawest most vulnerable love for this girl.

"I'll go to Percé tomorrow and see him," I croaked.

She linked her arm in mine and we began to walk down the field among the haycocks, both of us embarrassed by all the feeling that had been laid bare between us. Then she cried, "Look." She was pointing at an enormous orange moon that was rising out of the sea, flooding the bay with light. We stopped to watch its rising.

"It's a big bugger, isn't it?" she said. "Just look at that."

And it was something to behold, a luminous, elemental presence, governing tidal waters, arresting thought, filling us both with a momentary wonder.

Odette said, "Do you know what?"

"What?"

"My father is coming for a visit in ten days. I can't wait."

"When was the last time you saw him?"

"Last Christmas."

"That's good, Odette," I said. "I'm glad you'll get to see him."

"You'll like him, James," she said. "I'll introduce you. My father likes to speak to English people."

The awkwardness between us had passed, and she gave me a little push before we parted.

"That was a nice present you gave my brother," she said.

Adam had dressed him with considerable panache in dark trousers, white shirt, and a black-and-grey checked jacket. Tucked around his throat was a blue silk handkerchief, *un foulard de soie*. Gabriel's long white hair had been brushed and the pallor of his cheeks brightened by rouge, though that cosmetic agent must surely be called something else nowadays. The old word put me in mind of my mother dressing for a dinner party on a Saturday evening, seated at the mirror in her bedroom and applying colour to her face with a tiny brush. When I was a little boy, she never minded my watching her dress, and often talked about how she would much rather stay at home and read a story to me but she had also to think of my father. How I hated the notion of sharing her with him!

Seated by the window Gabriel welcomed me cheerily.

"Come in, James, come in, come in, come in," he called. Evidently the morphine suppositories were doing their work.

The suite was opulent, as you might expect, but very warm, and I knew I would soon have to remove my jacket. Adam was dressed for a tropical night, in slacks, a yellow polo shirt, and penny loafers. The hotel people had wheeled in a table laden with food: a tureen of what looked like *vichyssoise*, a platter of cold cuts and salads, yogourt and fruit. There were vases of fresh flowers on tables and on the mantel an uncorked bottle of champagne in an ice bucket. Adam gave me a glass of wine and I joined Gabriel by the window, which offered essentially the same view as the one from my room a floor below, though you could see a little farther over the trees of the park to the lake and mountains beyond. Gabriel was looking out at it all, and I wondered what thoughts were passing through his mind on his last evening. And then, incongruously, my thoughts turned to some other room in that little Swiss city, a room much less grand certainly, perhaps in the student quarter, where my golden-haired Heidi was sleeping beside her scruffy boyfriend, the two of them beneath a single sheet, naked and exhausted after their erotic exertions. I imagined the early evening light falling across her face and bare shoulders, wondered too at what point the imagination simply gives up on sex and leaves the old in peace.

I saw Gabriel wince, shifting slightly in his chair, an arrow of pain maybe getting past the morphine. He sipped some champagne.

"I've been telling Adam about our summer together in Quebec during the war," he said. "Long before he saw the light of day, eh, James?"

"Yes, Gabriel. It was a long time ago."

"I was telling him how you used to come over to the hotel from that village you lived in. You used to come with your uncle."

"Yes, Uncle Chester."

"He was queer as a duck's foot that man, and when I told our young friend here, why his ears perked right up. He likes to hear about queer folk like himself."

Adam was obviously accustomed to this sort of comment and smiled absently as he looked over things at the food table.

"Your uncle had a funny little car," Gabriel said.

"Yes, a Willys from the late thirties."

"The Willys Company," said Gabriel, "made trucks and jeeps for the army during the war. My father had shares in that company and he did all right. Say, that girl I had a fling with that summer, Yvette. She was a hot little number. You liked her too, didn't you?"

"Yes, I did like her."

"But she liked me. We used to fuck like anything. As soon as my mother left the room, Yvette would come in and we'd go at it like polecats."

The old man's lewd words made me want to clap my hands against my ears. I could see that Adam too was embarrassed. I couldn't help myself.

"Do you remember the picnic we went on, Gabriel? The four of us, you and me and the two girls? It rained and your wheelchair got stuck in the middle of a field."

He was staring out the window again, sipping his champagne.

"No, I don't recall a picnic. I remember a boat ride. We went around that big island in a boat to see all the birds. I had a pair of binoculars and you and I were looking for German submarines."

Either he had truly forgotten the day of the picnic, or he had simply edited the disgraceful behaviour from his memory. But what did it matter anyway? The man was dying and I had to behave better in his company.

"I liked your mother, Gabriel," I said. "I hope she had a long and happy life."

He smirked at that. As if my words evinced some hopeless ignorance of the ways of the world.

"Mother left us," he said. "Not long after that summer in Quebec—a couple of years. The war was over. Yes, I was in my first year at college when she ran off with the cowboy."

As he sipped his champagne, Gabriel seemed bitterly amused by the memory. "She met this fellow at a dude ranch out in California. He'd been an actor in B pictures. Mostly cowboy movies. 'Westerns' we used to call them. His name was Chip. Chip Meadows. Made up of course. Big rugged guy. Born to look good on a horse. He was in some of those Hop-along Cassidy movies. Do you remember those?"

"I do. We used to watch them on Saturday afternoons."

"By then Chip was out of the movie business and running this dude ranch, and according to my father, Chip and Mother used to spend a lot of time riding together. You have to under-stand that my father was fifteen years older than Mother and I guess he couldn't keep up with her in the old razzmatazz. Anyway, she left us. Wrote me a nice letter about her feelings for Chip, and how these things sometimes happen in life. I visited them once. This was a couple of years after they got married. I remember it was my first time on a plane and we stopped in Chicago to refuel. They met me at the airport in L.A. and took me down to the ranch in Chip's Lincoln convertible. Sun on our faces and the wind blowing in our hair. But nothing much to do at a dude ranch for a young fellow in a wheelchair. Still, I had eyes in my head and I could see that what was going on between Mother and Chip wasn't going to last. Too much drinking. Too much squabbling. I was glad to get the hell out of there. Anyway, a couple of years later, Mother disappeared."

"Disappeared?"

"Yes, she disappeared. Vanished off the face of the earth. The story was in some of those detective magazines that were popular then. This was in the early fifties. She and Chip went down to Mexico for a holiday. They stayed with one of Chip's old movie pals who had this house right on the edge of the desert. And one night at a party, Chip and my mother had one of their quarrels and she walked out. Walked out onto the patio and kept going, heading straight out into that desert in the dark of night. People said she was pretty drunk. And that was it. Nobody ever laid eyes on her again. Not a trace. Of course, the Mexican cops are hopeless at solving any crime, especially if it involves a visitor to their goddamn country. They didn't have a clue. For a while they considered Chip a suspect, but he had the perfect alibi. Some woman said he was in her bed all night. So to this day nobody knows what happened. My father hired a private detective and spent about twenty thousand dollars trying to find out. And that was a helluva lot of money in 1953.

But nothing. Not a damn thing. As I said, the old mater vanished off the face of the earth."

"That's incredible."

"It is, isn't it," he said gloomily. "A long time ago. They wrote about it in those detective magazines for a while and then it was forgotten."

"Maybe," I began, but he was already looking over at Adam, asking for some yogourt.

"I like the peach best, Adam."

Embittered amusement at the memory of his mother had given way to brooding. I was sorry I had raised the subject. Adam was now standing over him with a spoonful of yogourt.

"Give me that," Gabriel said. "I can still feed myself, for Christ's sake."

To make his point, he took the dish and crammed two spoonfuls of yogourt into his mouth, leaving a white smear on his upper lip. Adam seemed to consider wiping it away, but must have decided against it.

"Would you like me to get you something to eat, sir?" he asked me. "Another glass of champagne?"

"I'll help myself," I said, and going over to the buffet I put a few things on a plate. I hadn't eaten much that day, but still had little appetite. Gabriel was watching me carefully as I carried my plate back to a chair near the window.

He waited for me to sit down and then asked, "Do you ever think about the end, James?"

"Yes," I said, "from time to time I do."

"It's bound to happen to you one of these days," he said. "You're what now, seventy-five?"

"Not quite. I'll be seventy-five next February."

"Well, there you are, then. It catches us all in time."

"Indeed it does."

"Does it bother you?" he asked.

"Not particularly."

Adam had deftly reached down with a napkin and wiped the old man's mouth, and this irritated Gabriel, for he waved his hand at the dish in his lap.

"Take it, take it, take it. I've had enough of this. What did you say you did for a living, James?"

"I was a professor of English literature," I said. "The Victorians. Tennyson and his contemporaries."

He nodded. "I don't suppose you see anything on the other side?"

"I think it highly unlikely," I said, and this opinion was met with a bark of laughter.

"Highly unlikely," said Gabriel. "I like that. Not altogether, but on the other hand perhaps, though maybe not. Why do I think that that's the sort of fellow you turned out to be? I believe I saw some of that in you when we were boys together."

How prescient the old ruffian was! I'd underestimated him, for I did indeed turn out to be that kind of man.

Gabriel was looking at Adam. "But do you know what, James? Our young friend here believes in it. Yes sir. He and his friend think there might be something on the other side. What's your pal's name, Adam?"

"Donald, sir."

"Yes, Donald. Adam told me they'd like to get married one day. Isn't that something, now?"

Why, I wondered, was he bothering himself at this hour with Adam Trench's beliefs and sexual inclination? What did it matter? I supposed it was just habit, his customary mockery of things he didn't approve of, but it struck me as a sad and remarkable fact, that even dying we can put forth our worst face. Gabriel was now staring down at the carpet with that intensely inward look of the mortally ill who must from time to time concede everything to pain. After a moment, he looked up and smiled, and even in that ravaged old face were signs of the handsomeness I remembered.

"I wanted," he said, "to talk to you about that summer in Quebec, James. It was a happy time in my life. Maybe my happiest, when I think of it. That's why I was so glad to see you in London the other day. But goddamn it, I'm just not up to it. I'm not even close."

Raising an arm he pointed, and stepping behind the chair Adam wheeled him towards the bathroom, from where I soon heard the retching.

For a few minutes I stood by the window looking out at the street lights through the dark trees, thinking of Susan and what lay ahead of her. When Gabriel returned he gave me another weak smile.

"My apologies, but this dying is an ugly business. By this time tomorrow, however, it'll all be over and you and Adam can have a bang-up meal on me." Reaching back he patted Adam's hand. "He's a good fellow. I know I give him a hard time, but he'll be well rewarded." He looked up at him. "Now what about tomorrow? Have you filled in James on what transpires in the morning?"

Adam looked directly at me. "We are expected at ten o'clock, sir. The taxi will pick us up at nine-thirty and the ride will take approximately twenty minutes."

"Have you got that, James? Nine-thirty."

"I have."

"Good, good, good. Have some more champagne, for Christ's sake. And something to eat. Look at all this food. Don't let it go to waste. Now, James, I'm sorry, but I just feel like hell and I think I'll go to bed. The stuff I'm taking tires you out. Help yourself here now."

"No, Gabriel," I said, "I think I'll call it a day too and go back to my room."

He shrugged. "Suit yourself. See you in the morning." He was already waving Adam onward towards a bedroom.

When I returned to my room, I sat down and tried to remember as much as I could of an evening almost a year before, the last Sunday in November. I had planned a dinner to celebrate Susan's appointment as the sixteenth headmistress of Woolford Abbey. She would be leaving Canada on Boxing Day, and I didn't want my dinner freighted with all the emotional baggage of the holiday season. The previous Christmas had been chaotic, with the two children shuttled back and forth between the family home and David and Nikki's condominium, Brian still bewildered by the absence of his father in daily life, and Gillian fighting with her mother in one house and glaring at her father and his young "partner" in another. With the passing of nearly a year, matters had improved: Brian was now more accustomed to the ways of adults and Gillian had found Jermaine; Brenda was finding her way and had plans to resume her nursing career in some form or another. She was taking university courses, and I was pleased for her, hoping that perhaps a lonely, sensible middle-aged man was somewhere in her future. Still, I was taking no chances; this was to be Susan's evening and there would be just eight of us: Brenda and the two children, David but not Nikki, who supposedly was in New York on business. True or not, I didn't care, it was simpler this way. Susan with her best friend, Sophie Wasserman, my friend Catherine Parmeter, and myself.

I had chosen an ordinary Sunday at the end of November. Ordinary, that is, for most people, though as Catherine reminded me, it was the First Sunday of Advent and so she wanted to attend Evensong. It would be five weeks later in Bermuda that Catherine would tell me she was going on her sabbatical to Auckland the following summer. In her own way, she was bidding farewell. On that November Sunday, however, I went to Evensong with her, for as I've mentioned, I enjoy the music and the language of these services. Catherine, in turn, agreed to help me with dinner, though frankly I'm better in the kitchen than she is; Catherine's idea of helping out is to lean against the kitchen counter and chat while I peel potatoes. She's never had much interest in food or its preparation. Over a lifetime, she's eaten most of her meals in restaurants or in university cafeterias. As far as she is concerned, french fries and gravy will do as well as anything, and a pork roast dinner with potatoes and turnips is the best meal of all. Poetry and sex and her Anglo-Catholic faith have been enough to sustain her during this earthly course, as she playfully calls life.

So we went to the church with its anthems and candlelit

shadows and the old words; on one side of me Catherine's austere and still quite striking profile, and on the other my granddaughter's youthful beauty. Gillian's presence was a genuine surprise, for she'd never shown the slightest interest in religion. But that afternoon she'd phoned to ask if she could come along. And there she was dressed for the occasion in a skirt and white blouse over which she wore a cape. With her blond ponytailed hair, she looked fetching enough to capture even the admiring glances of the many gay men in attendance. Gillian told me she hadn't been inside a church since a brief infatuation with Sunday school when she was nine or ten. But that Sunday she took everything in with the impassive look of teenagers who in adult company do not want to appear too impressed.

Afterwards I asked her what she thought of it and she said it was "neat," a catch-all adjective that signifies approval if nothing else. I think though that Gillian may have accompanied us also because she was always intrigued by Catherine and the idea that I had a girlfriend. That too she found "neat." But she was particularly drawn to Catherine's way of getting on in the world, to the self-assurance, the unruffled nature that was so unlike her mother's and her own. Older calmer spirits are often attractive to the young. I used to notice how female students followed Catherine from her classroom to her office doorway, eager for guidance or advice.

When we left the church, it was a mild dark evening with a light rain, almost a mist in the air. A Dickensian evening that suited me perfectly, for soon we would be indoors where food and drink and warmth awaited us. It's never lost on me how my boyhood reading of Dickens' novels has left me with these quaint notions of creature comforts. How his descriptions of food and the family table and the contrasting images of coach rides on rainy nights or damp, foggy streets beyond curtained windows have coloured my imagination. And some of it at least was there when we got back from church. The large capon I had dressed that afternoon was out of the oven and cooling on the counter. Brenda had prepared the vegetables and salad. The day before, I had bought a rich elaborate cake from an Italian bakery on St. Clair Avenue. The wine was uncorked and there was talk and laughter in my apartment. Susan and Sophie and David had surrounded my grandson, and were questioning him about school and video games and a recent trip to the Science Centre. Brian, who is diffident at times, seemed pleased by the attention. On the sofa Catherine was explaining to Gillian the concept of Advent, a term Gillian hadn't heard until that afternoon. As I set the table, I caught David casting looks at Brenda, who was helping me. There was still some heavy lifting to do in the divorce proceedings, but according to Brenda (David never talked to me about the details), it was beginning to look as if everything would be settled by spring. Brenda would keep the house; she'd insisted on that and apparently David had no objections. Frankly I had worried about the two of them together that evening; a few months earlier it would have been a disaster, but now it looked as if they could at least bear each other's company for a few hours.

Susan looked terrific in a smart pantsuit and blouse, the very outfit, when I think of it, that she would wear eleven months later when we had dinner in that little French restaurant in Woolford. During her last year at St. Hilda's, she had been watching her weight, swimming every morning in the pool. Beside her, Sophie seemed her old self, and by that I mean that for many years her good nature had been partly submerged in a bad marriage. But since its breakup she had recovered almost completely. Her neurotic and useless husband, a want-to-be novelist whom she supported and nurtured through a dozen years, was gone, living in Vancouver where he was making another woman's life miserable. Sophie told me she was still paying his psychiatrist's bills. But free at last from looking after the creep, she was flourishing again and, as she told me, had decided to be what she was always meant to be, a happy, fat woman. So she favours large floral dresses, loose blouses and long skirts, pearls and beads and sometimes a bandana for her rich auburn hair. The grande dame look, a bit operatic but it suits her, and that evening she was wearing an orange floral-print dress and she looked, I thought, resplendent.

From time to time I've wondered about Susan and Sophie. About their lifelong friendship, I mean. Was there anything sexual in it? Not that it matters one way or another, but I couldn't help wondering over the years. Now I'm inclined to doubt it. I don't know about Sophie, but I'm convinced that Susan is determinedly heterosexual.

When younger she had her share of boyfriends, and in her twenties she met the love of her life, a young doctor from Israel. He was in fact Sophie's cousin, and it was Sophie who introduced them. Abel Wasserman was a pediatrician at the Hospital for Sick Children, newly arrived from the Holy Land, as my mother used to call that beleaguered country. Abel was good-looking and apparently brilliant in his field. Yet I couldn't warm to the man. Perhaps I detected in him something that Susan couldn't or wouldn't see, an overly ambitious and calculating approach to life. But she was simply overwhelmed by him. At least for a while. Sophie of course was delighted. But I worried about how it would all work out, and so I was the least surprised when after two years Dr. Wasserman abruptly broke off the relationship. It seems there had been another woman in his life for some time, another doctor, and they eventually went off to California together. A new life in another land, and maybe that had been the idea all along. Susan was devastated, and I can still remember how her ruthless and unconquerable misery lay like a weight on my heart during most of one spring and the following summer. Sophie was there for her, but she too must have had misgivings about the role she played in something that just went wrong. But that was many years ago, and as we never tire of reminding ourselves, time heals. And it does, it's true. So listening to their laughter in my living room a year ago, I was carried back to our family home and the same laughter curling down the stairs from two sixteen-year-olds in Susan's bedroom.

I remember looking at all of them that November evening as Brenda and I served the food and refilled glasses. There around the dining room table were the people I loved, safe at least for the moment from the perils beyond the window. For Susan it was a moment of sheer triumph. She had secured at last the job she had long sought and everything now lay before her. It was true that I would no longer see as much of her. She would be in another country, but so what? England was only six hours away. I was already planning several trips a year. And there was always e-mail. We could be in touch within minutes. So she looked deservedly exultant that evening, and because she was happy, so was I. Yet there in the midst of that convivial hour, in the darkness of her body, the cancer cells were already dividing and multiplying, reaching out to grasp whatever lay in their path.

There was no escaping such grim thoughts. Cancer was again a leading player in my own narrative, the "heavy," who after an absence of twenty years had appeared again ten days ago. I would now go to sleep thinking about it, and a few hours later awaken to it; in between, as likely as not, I would dream about it, for isn't that the way our minds work during these ordeals, turning over and over the same assailing thoughts, maddening and exhausting us. Meanwhile the body must still look after itself; its daily needs cannot be forgotten for long. In Zurich it was nearly nine o'clock and I was hungry. Absurd, in a way, after being so close to all that food in Gabriel's suite. A terrible waste, no doubt, but I couldn't go to bed hungry, and so from Room Service I ordered a chicken sandwich and had that with a half-bottle of hock from the mini-bar.

When I tried David's number in Toronto, I again got only Nikki Martin's fiercely cheerful voice urging me to have yet another absolutely super day. So it was on to Brenda's, and thank goodness she was there, surprised and delighted to hear from me.

"Jim, are you really in Switzerland? Brian gave me the message yesterday and at first I wondered if he got it right, but then I said to myself, how could he make that up? What are you doing there, anyway?"

I explained the situation with Gabriel, and after hearing me out, she gave a low, soft whistle of wonderment.

"You're really getting it, aren't you. First Susan and now this? How is Susan, anyway? God, I've wanted to phone her, but I've been waiting to hear from you. Or maybe I'm just afraid to talk to her. I'm not so good one-on-one with Susan, you know that."

This unfortunately was true. Brenda has always felt intimidated by Susan and this has puzzled my daughter because she has never wanted it to be like that. She's fond of Brenda and has always tried to make her feel at ease. Sometimes, however, in spite of our best efforts, we can never reach a comfortable level with a particular person.

"It's serious, I'm afraid," I said. "Very serious. She's undergoing surgery in a couple of weeks. From now on she'll be in for a rough time."

"That's for sure. What rotten luck. And now you've got to deal with this old friend of yours?"

"Yes. Tomorrow morning he's going to take something that will kill him."

"You're going to watch this man die tomorrow morning?"

"Yes."

"Jesus Christ, Jim. Isn't that asking a lot from someone you haven't seen in sixty years?"

"Maybe, but Gabriel has no one else here except the young man who's been looking after him. A nice fellow, but he's still just hired help. It seems Gabriel has no family, no friends except me and I don't really know if I'm much of a friend. But I guess I'm all he's got. Anyway, he's thought it all through. It's his choice. Actually he's looking forward to it and I can't say that I blame him. He's in terrible shape. Pancreatic cancer."

"Yeah. Well, pancreatic cancer is a real bastard. I've seen it at work. It usually takes you out pretty fast, though it's hard to tell with any cancer. Some linger, some don't. But suicide?"

"It's all legal, Brenda. They do that kind of thing over here."

"Yeah, I've heard about it."

"Enlightened in a way, though it does make you a bit uneasy, whatever your feelings are on the subject."

"No kidding."

I could hear a sudden blast of sound. Not exactly music, but something like it perhaps, raucous and cheerful. It set Brenda yelling.

"Brian, turn that damn thing down. I'm on the phone with Grandpa. He's calling from Switzerland."

I thought I could hear a little voice in the background.

"Sorry about that, Jim. Brian says hi."

"Brenda, I hope you won't tell the children why I'm over here."

"I wasn't planning to, no."

"With their aunt's illness and everything, it could be unsettling for them."

"Yeah, I can see that."

"And David," I said. "I've tried to reach him but he's out. I'm not sure I would have told him exactly what I've been telling you. You know how David can be. So if you're talking to him, it's best if you just say that I'm in Switzerland to visit an old friend. Which after all is not exactly a lie."

"I doubt if I'll be talking to him before you get back. He sometimes calls about the kids. Arranging times to meet them. That sort of thing. But sure, if he calls I won't mention any of this stuff."

I said, "It's just that David would probably see this as excessively morbid behaviour. I don't think he'd quite understand."

"Well, I'm sure you're right about that," she said. "David is not exactly the most sympathetic person in the world."

I didn't want to take this any further. Didn't like the idea of going behind my son's back to discuss his shortcomings.

"Your reason for being in Switzerland is safe with me, Jim."

"Thanks."

"Frankly, I think it's a bit weird myself, but I can also see it as an act of friendship and I respect that."

I wasn't so sure about it being an "act of friendship," but I let that pass. I was touched by the concern I could hear in her voice.

"Brenda, I just wanted to talk to somebody tonight. This city, the atmosphere, the whole thing has . . ."

"Creeped you out?"

"Well, yes." I was laughing a little. "I've not heard that expression before."

"Oh, it's one of Gillian's. She uses it to describe horror movies or some classmate she finds ugly or unlikeable. Kids, you know. When are you coming home, anyway?"

"Tuesday."

197

"What time?"

"Two o'clock."

"I can pick you up. No, wait. Tuesday? Tuesday is a P.D. day for Brian, I think, but that's all right. He can come along. We'll both welcome you home."

"You needn't bother, Brenda. I can take a cab."

"I know you can take a cab, Jim, but don't be silly. Save your money. We'll pick you up. What airline are you using?"

"Air Canada."

"No problem. We'll be there."

"You're a gem, Brenda."

"Yeah right, a gem. A zircon, you mean."

It felt good to laugh with her.

"How is Gillian?"

"Gillian is Gillian. Right now she's with Jermaine. It's still Jermaine, Jermaine, Jermaine. I'm living through this. The months of the living dead. At least we no longer shout at each other. We just hiss now and then. The old mother snake and her teenage daughter."

"I'm sure it's not that bad."

"Maybe not. Rites of passage and all that bull."

"I'll go now, Brenda. I'm glad we talked. You've helped."

"Get through tomorrow and then get the hell out of there."

"I will."

"See you Tuesday, Jim."

By the middle of August 1944, the Germans were retreating eastward and their flight from Paris, which I read about in my uncle's newspapers, seemed already like a symbolic victory. Uncle Chester, who had never been to Europe, was nevertheless particularly enlivened at the prospect of the great city being freed from under the boot of the Hun, as he put it, his florid writing style sometimes creeping into conversation when he grew excited. I used to listen to him talking with the Porters on the veranda of the St. Lawrence Hotel, smoking his pipe furiously, pointing the stem from time to time at Sam Porter for emphasis. But Uncle Chester was right in a way. Such was our collective image of Paris (even at my age I felt it) as a centre of art and culture and learning that to imagine it liberated from the barbarians was inspiring. And I'm sure I caught some of the effervescence that was in the air. Yes, I had lost Odette to Gabriel Fontaine, but I think I was inclined by then to see myself as a casualty in another kind of war, a soldier in the vast army of the unrequited. And that, along with a

softer light and a shorter day, foretold the end of summer. I'm
sure I was often filled with a pleasing melancholy.

The end of summer also meant a return to school. In spite
of my carping about Groveland, I was beginning to miss the
quirky teachers, the companionship of boys my age, the comforting rituals of school life. Now that I knew the ropes, I could
tell newcomers where to find things and whom to see about
this or that. With the authority granted the returning student,
I could now boss around younger boys or dispense my dol-
lop of mercy as I saw fit. I was anticipating these heady times.
With the end of summer, we would all be leaving, Gabriel
and Mrs. Fontaine, the Porters, and myself. All except Uncle
Chester, who would be staying on for another month, working on Billy Benson's adventures. I knew he would be glad to
see the end of us. From chance remarks I could tell that he
was growing tired of the bridge games and tennis matches, of
Mr. Porter's endless observations on how the Americans were
winning the war for the rest of us; I think he was even growing tired of Eleanor Fontaine's exuberant optimism and her
persistent need to be admired.

I was beginning to see that my uncle was not exactly the
preposterous figure I had always thought him to be at family
gatherings, an exotic show-off with a cruel tongue. When first
I had heard that I would be spending the summer with him, I
had gone at once to my mother's bookshelf upstairs and leafed
through *Roget's Thesaurus* in search of a term to describe him,
settling finally on *popinjay*. It had a Victorian ring that I recognized even then, a word that Alfred T might well have used to
describe an enemy. I was delighted by its sound and its descrip-

tive encompassment of conceited ass. Knowing the word, say-ing it aloud to myself from time to time, heartened me for the weeks ahead. Yet by the end of that summer, I was seeing Uncle Chester in a different light. Still a popinjay, yes—there was no changing that—but something more; he was also witty and intelligent, aware that the world was not to be confronted uncritically, that it abounded with charlatans and fools, and one had constantly to be on guard. In a way, this revised assess-ment of him was disconcerting, for I was now able to see ele-ments of myself in Uncle Chester. We were far more alike in temperament and attitude than I had previously imagined; moreover, with the passing weeks a subtle change had taken place between us. We seemed more patient with each other's imperfections, less likely to exchange snide mockeries or sar-castic asides. We had unwittingly achieved a kind of détente. Either that, or we recognized similarities within ourselves and decided that we liked each other a little better than we had thought. We'd even adopted a sly complicity in deflecting some of Mrs. Moore's slow-witted approaches to conversation. Sometimes we behaved more or less like two clever school-boys having fun at the expense of a dull classmate.

On the last Saturday of the month, Uncle Chester and I were at lunch, being served Mrs. Moore's nourishing vegeta-ble soup. As she placed the soup before us she announced that "The father came in on the train today." Mrs. Moore had an oblique way of conveying information: news was shorn of any context, with no allusive hint of how it might be connected to something that had already been mentioned. It was as if she expected the listener to read her mind and sort out everything himself as he parsed the information. I knew this habit irritated my uncle, but he usually dealt with it by inserting the occasional *Is that so?* or *You don't say?* hiding as always behind his *Quebec Chronicle-Telegraph* or the week-old *Globe and Mail*. By late August, however, he was clearly worn down by it all and his tendency to be sarcastic was surfacing. When Mrs. Moore, for instance, said "The father came in on the train today," Uncle Chester settled the paper on his lap, and looking down at his soup, greeted her cryptic observation by saying, "And pray, whose father might that be, Mrs. Moore?" You could safely play that card with Mrs. Moore, whose matter-of-fact, solid-brick disposition was impervious to mockery. That my uncle's little darts could not pierce the landlady's armour didn't seem to bother him. Merely firing them seemed to be enough.

"Next door," explained Mrs. Moore. "The Huards. He came in on today's train. I saw him walking up the lane with his suitcase while I was in the garden. He must be home for a holiday. They say he works in a factory in Montreal."

"Is that so?" said my uncle.

"They say he makes a good wage, but he certainly doesn't give much of it to that poor soul."

My uncle looked up from his soup. "What poor soul, Mrs. Moore?"

"Her. The wife. Mrs. Huard. Why, she hasn't a decent dress to go to church in. And you've seen the children?"

"Actually, I haven't," said Uncle Chester, who was cooling a spoonful of soup by lightly blowing on it. "Not up close at any rate. If it comes to that, I haven't had much to do with the Huard family. Nothing, to be exact."

Yet if Uncle Chester wasn't the least bit interested in the comings and goings of our neighbours, I certainly was, and the arrival of Mr. Huard was news. Since first hearing about him from Odette, I had been looking forward to seeing this paragon of fatherhood, this former seminarian and progenitor of eight who toiled for his family in a munitions factory. Because I was usually perched near the window gazing across the field, I can't imagine how I missed seeing him walk up the lane, unless that morning I was absorbed in *Great Expectations*. I was reading the novel slowly, making sure to leave just enough for the train ride back to Toronto. I'm sure I thought it would be fitting if I finished the book just before we reached Union Station. Who can explain these small, peculiar compulsions we live with, though perhaps *compulsions* is too clinical a term for what, after all, are fairly harmless foibles.

That Saturday afternoon, I watched the children gather around their father, who sat on the steps of the gallery. Even Mrs. Huard, that pale ghost of a woman, came out and sat on a kitchen chair for a few minutes with the baby settled on her lap. Mr. Huard had brought gifts for the children, and one of them was pushing a little car or truck across the yard. Mr. Huard smoked and watched his family. When Odette had talked about her father, I'd pictured a burly man, someone used to handling artillery shells on a factory floor, but Olivier Huard was slight and, from my window, looked much younger than I'd imagined. In his trousers and white shirt with the sleeves rolled up past his elbows, he seemed more like a schoolteacher or a bookkeeper than a factory hand. As I learned later that day, that's exactly what he was, a bookkeeper.

I don't know why this disappointed me, unless I felt at the time
that bookkeeping had less to do with winning the war than
filling or stacking artillery shells. So I knelt by the window,
glancing now and then at a few more pages of Pip's infatuation with the icy-hearted Estelle. I didn't want to miss Odette
coming up the lane. I was anxious to see her joy as she set eyes
upon her father.

As the afternoon wore on, the Huard children too began
looking for her, and when the little truck stopped on the highway, they were already running down the lane with the collie, shouting, "*Odette, Odette, Papa est ici.*" Surrounding her, they
tugged at her arms with excited cries. When Odette saw her
father she waved, and Olivier Huard raised an arm in greeting
from the gallery. As she drew closer to the house, though, I
could see her steps quickening and then she broke from the
children and ran. Her father got up then, brushing the seat of
his trousers with one hand and flicking away his cigarette with
the other. Walking towards her he opened his arms and into
them she ran, and he whirled her around and around. I could
hear their laughter in the hot, still afternoon. When they finished embracing, they went arm in arm into the house and the
children followed. Only the black-and-white dog remained
on the gallery, still revved up by the commotion, pacing back
and forth before settling finally by the door and stretching
out to sleep. Later I watched Odette and her father walking
down the lane together. She was wearing a white blouse and
plaid slacks that I'd not seen before, and I guessed they were
gifts from her father. The new clothes made her look more
like the young women I saw on the streets of Toronto. As they

walked along the highway towards the village, her father was gesturing with his hands as she listened, and I felt obscurely jealous. What was he telling her? I wondered. Had he found a house for them in Montreal? Would she soon be leaving the village too?

That evening I walked across the field to see her. I was curious about Olivier Huard and I was hoping she would introduce me to him. I also wanted to know if she had overheard the quarrel between Gabriel and his mother. What did she think of her hero now, after listening to all that? To please her I had done as she had asked on that evening when we watched the harvest moon rising from the sea; on afternoons I had started again to go with my uncle to Percé, to walk up the wide stairs of the hotel to Gabriel's room, his "pal" once more. But on the day before Olivier Huard's arrival, I was stopped outside Gabriel's door by the sound of an argument. He and his mother were shouting at each other. Anyone passing in the hallway could have heard them. He was calling his mother names, a cheapskate, a drunk, an old bag, and she in turn was calling him a goddamn little thief. Money was missing from her handbag. "If you want money, you should ask for it," she yelled. It was embarrassing to listen to, and I didn't see how I could knock on the door and interrupt such a scene, so I went back down to the veranda where Uncle Chester and Mr. and Mrs. Porter were sitting—"Waiting for Eleanor who is always late," according to my uncle. Ten minutes later mother and son appeared, and had I not known, I never could have guessed that they had so recently been at each other's throats. As she pushed Gabriel's chair towards us,

Mrs. Fontaine leaned across his shoulder and said something that made him laugh.

Gabriel and I set out for the wharf that afternoon, but it began to rain and we returned to his room, where we listened to dance-band music and played cribbage for a penny a point. Gabriel won nearly every game and was his old exuberant self in victory. To keep me happy he played records he knew I liked, Bunny Berrigan's "I Can't Get Started" and Artie Shaw's "Begin the Beguine." He offered me his Camels, but I was tired of smoking. Had decided it wasn't worth the trouble. All that afternoon I felt uneasy in Gabriel's company, and I think it had to do with the Fontaines themselves: the violence of their emotions, the ease and dispatch with which they moved from exhilaration to rage. All that feeling on display. It bothered me, and I'm sure Gabriel thought I was something of a wet blanket that day. I left him mulling over the jigsaw puzzle with Tommy Dorsey. I wanted to know what Odette thought of her hero stealing from his mother's purse.

The Huards were used to me now. Even the dog no longer barked at my approach but only jumped about, sniffing my legs and letting me pass into the yard. Odette must have been watching from the window as I crossed the field, for she came out onto the gallery and was joined by her father, who surprised me by coming down the steps and holding out his hand.

"Hello there, James," he said, as if we were old friends. "Odette has told me all about you."

We shook hands and I said hello, but I could think of little else. I was thrown by Olivier Huard's familiar manner. It wasn't the way you expected a man in those days to talk to a boy. It put us on a footing I wasn't used to. Odette was watching us from the gallery.

"Odette has told me you are from Toronto," he said. "I've never been to Toronto, but I plan to someday. Once this war is over, I'm thinking I will leave Quebec and move to Ontario. It's good to speak English. I don't get a chance to practise my English enough."

All this sudden, rapid-fire information about himself seemed odd to me.

"Your English is fine, Mr. Huard," I said. "Better than my French."

"Ah, well," he said. "Not as good as it might be, I bet."

He was not much taller than I was, lean and dark-haired, boyishly handsome. He didn't look like the father of eight children, but more like a bachelor uncle, a favourite of the family who had dropped by for a visit. He was eager to know more about me: what kind of school did I go to and what did my father do? And what about my uncle who wrote books? Was there a good living in that line of work? I answered his questions without making too much of my father's job in Ottawa. My faults as a boy were plentiful enough, but boastfulness was not among them, and always I kept in mind the words of my mother as we parted on my first day at Groveland School. "Always remember, James," she said on that September afternoon, "that you and the other boys at this school are more fortunate than most but that's really just a matter of luck and nothing to brag about." My father was waiting in the car, and I wondered what he would have made of her comment. But I took it to heart, for it suited my disposition.

I wasn't sure whether Olivier Huard's childlike curiosity was ingenuous or merely ingratiating, but it did strike me that he seemed too eager to please a fourteen-year-old boy, and I think I saw in him a man who perhaps lived on promises that were seldom fulfilled. I wondered too if during his questioning of me Odette saw any of this, for I remember she began to look uncomfortable, even a little cross.

"I think James and I will go for a walk, Papa," she said.

"Yes, yes, that's good," he said. "You go for a walk with James. It's a beautiful evening for walking. No rain in that sky, I bet." He was looking up, scanning the heavens as if inviting agreement.

Odette and I walked down the lane in silence and there was a poignancy to all this that I cannot describe. Somehow Odette seemed disappointed in both her father and in me. In the evening light, we walked along the highway through the village to the cove. I knew we wouldn't have many more walks together.

When we reached the cove we sat on our favourite log and looked out at the sea. She finally said, "My father is pretty nosy, isn't he."

"That's all right," I said, "he's just curious about people. There's nothing wrong with that."

"Maybe not," she said. "Anyway, he says he's got a house for us. In St-Henri. Do you know Montreal, James?"

"No."

She was doing what she often did when we sat together on that log, leaning forward to scoop up a handful of sand, then letting it spill through her fingers.

"It's a poor part of the city," she said. "What do you say in English when the head is filled with lice?"

"It's lousy," I said.

"Yes, it's lousy. I've heard that word. And you use it to describe things that aren't good. So we're going to a *lousy* neighbourhood, but it's all he can afford, I guess."

I asked her when they would be leaving for Montreal.

"I don't know," she said. "Sometime next month. I'm not going to start school here, I know that. I'm going to stay on at the hotel until we leave. My father knows somebody who has a car and he is going up to Montreal to see about a job. My father thinks he can get him a job and so some of us can go up with him. The others will go with my mother on the train. I don't know what they'll do with our furniture. Send it by truck or something. When we get there, we'll be late for classes. Other kids will look at us and say things to each other. They'll laugh behind their hands. It's always the same."

She got up from the log, brushing the seat of her new slacks just the way her father had brushed his outside their house. The afterglow from the sunset had left the sky a remarkably deep orange and this was reflected in the water, which looked like a painting, only with the colour changing by the moment. Odette sat down again, but then got up. She couldn't keep still.

"When are you going home?" she asked.

"A week from Tuesday," I said. "The day after Labour Day."

"Gabriel is leaving next Saturday," she said over her shoulder as she walked down to the shore, where she began to skip stones across that coloured water.

She threw the stones with a deft side motion, and I watched the little flashes of light in the darkening water. Then she turned and walked back towards me. How quickly the darkness had enfolded us. As she walked I could no longer see her face clearly; she was only a figure in a white blouse and dark pants.

When she sat on the log beside me she said, "Do you know what, James? I think I'm pregnant. I should have had the curse by now and anyway I feel funny."

"Funny?"

"Yes. Well, not funny in the way you think of the word, but different. I feel different. There's something going on inside me. My tits sometimes tingle." She leaned against me and took my arm. "Do you know about these things, James? About a girl's period and all that? The bees and the birds." She sounded almost amused, but I knew it was just an act.

"I'm sorry it's happened, Odette."

"Yes," she said, bending forward to pick up another handful of sand. "I am ... how do you say it in English? I am in a pickle. I have always thought that is a funny way to describe something serious. To be in a pickle."

"Have you told him?" I asked.

She laughed. "Told Gabriel? No." Her *no* was so adamant, so scornful. As if I had suggested something ridiculous. "What can he do about it?" she said. "Marry me? Take me back with him to the States? A rich kid like that. Why should he care if I'm pregnant?"

"You're only sixteen, Odette," I said.

"Actually not," she said. "I won't be sixteen until December.

Two days before Christmas. But so what? Fifteen, sixteen, I'm still pregnant. I'm pretty sure of that now."

"You should tell him," I said. "He's responsible."

She laughed again and squeezed my arm. "You are such a proper guy, James. I like that about you. Maybe you should have been the one to make me pregnant, eh? You would look after me, I bet."

"Yes, I would look after you." I sounded so earnest and it was easy enough to say, though I couldn't really imagine myself in such circumstances.

"Well," she said after a moment. "It wasn't all his fault. I didn't say no."

"You should tell him just the same," I said. "You should tell his mother too. They should help you out."

She was looking straight ahead, no longer holding my arm but hugging herself against the night air.

"They should, they should, they should. Who says they should? You? I can see me telling his mother. Sure I can. She'd love to hear the news, I bet."

"You have to tell them, Odette," I said. "It's not fair if they don't know."

She said nothing and we sat listening to the water lapping the shore. She then put her head on my shoulder. I could smell her hair, and I listened to her murmur, "*Merde, merde, merde.*"

"What are you going to do?" I asked. I liked the weight of her leaning against me.

"I don't know," she said dreamily, as if only half listening. "There are places to go. The Church has homes for people like me. The nuns look after you. I knew a girl once who went to one of these homes in Montreal."

"Have you told anyone else? Pauline?"

"No, she would just tell others. Pauline can't keep anything to herself. Piss on her. She will never know. I'll be gone from this *maudit* village by the time she finds out, if she ever does."

She was still talking as if half asleep, as if wearied by thinking of it all. Her head felt heavy on my shoulder, but I didn't care.

"You'll need money," I said. "Do you have any?"

"I have a little, yes."

"I can give you some," I said. "Maybe twenty-five dollars. I think I have that much."

She sat up, put her arm around me, and kissed my neck.

"You are a nice boy, James," she said, "but I don't want your money."

"I want you to have it," I said. "I don't need it. I'm going home soon. My ticket is paid for."

"No," she said.

I felt such outrage then. None of this was fair. He was going to get away with it.

"I'm going to tell Gabriel if you won't," I said.

She pulled away from me at once.

"Don't do that," she said. "Don't mention this to him. It does no good. He's got enough to think about."

"Like what?"

"Like the life ahead of him," she said. "Gabriel is a spoiled boy, but there is good in him too. I had lots of fun with him.

I should have been more careful. It's my fault too. I can't just blame him."

"He's a rich American show-off who cries like a baby when things don't go his own way. You saw him that day we had the picnic. Yelling like that."

Odette was shaking her head. "You are such a blamer, James. It's blame, blame, blame all the time. Why are you like that? Gabriel can't help being the way he is. He's proud. I told you before. He didn't want to be carried like that. Like a child in the arms of that stupid bastard Emile, who just picked him up without a word. How would you like that to happen in front of your friends?"

I can't recall how I answered her question or even if I did. I know that I didn't mention the quarrel between Gabriel and his mother. That all seemed so petty now. For some reason, I can't even remember how that evening ended. We must have walked back from the cove together, but maybe not. Maybe I grew sulky over her loyalty to Gabriel and we returned by separate ways. We did that now and then after disagreeing, and that evening may have been one of those times.

When I saw her the next day at the St. Lawrence Hotel, however, we were friends again. We smiled at each other in the hallway. I remember that.

That Monday in Zurich, I awakened early after a fitful sleep. I was the first guest in the dining room and had my breakfast while reading a version of world events as reported by those who labour for the *International Herald Tribune*. Later I walked in the little park at the front of the hotel, looking out through the trees at the blue trolley cars and the early joggers on the pathway by the lake. Beyond all that were the distant Alps, emblems, as good as any, of Nature's lofty indifference to our various plights. The sun had burned away a mist over the lake. It was going to be another warm day for that time of year. Now and then I glanced back towards the hotel entrance, watching for Adam and Gabriel. At exactly nine-thirty, a van pulled into the driveway, and as it turned around, they came out of the hotel. One of the staff was holding the door for them. As I approached, Gabriel raised a hand in greeting.

"So there you are, James," he said. "I thought you might chicken out at the last minute. Adam and I had a bet on it, didn't we." He was looking up at Adam. "I owe you ten bucks, but I guess it doesn't really matter, does it. You'll be going through my pockets within the hour, you heartless thing."

"Don't worry about that, sir," Adam said.

Gabriel frowned. "I'm not worried about a goddamn thing, my boy. I just want to get this show on the road."

The driver had opened the door and set in motion the hydraulic contraption that lifted the wheelchair into the vehicle. I listened to its thrumming sound as Gabriel was adroitly placed within the van. Adam climbed in beside him, and I sat next to the driver.

The streets of the city had been freshly washed and now glistened in the sunlight. Where were we going? Where would Gabriel drink the poisoned cup? Adam had given the driver a piece of paper with the address, and no one spoke during the twenty minutes or so that it took to reach our destination, a dreary stretch of the suburban commonplace. The postcard streets of old Zurich were behind us now, and we were passing strip malls and apartment buildings and technology companies, the landscape of our times. Except for the low wooded hills on either side—Zurich was settled along a river valley—we could have been on the outskirts of Toronto or Minneapolis. We drove along a street past a schoolyard where the children were at recess, running and shouting at their games. Then down another street, to a house where we stopped. It was set back in a small courtyard, shrubbery bordering the property. A nondescript bungalow. I thought I saw the parting of a curtain in one of the front windows.

At the door we were met by a woman in her fifties, her

greying blond hair pulled back into a bun. She shook each of our hands as we entered the house. There was about the woman an air of courteous gravity that inspired confidence, that seemed to say *you are in good hands, you will be looked after*. She escorted us down a hall—the house was sparsely furnished as though no one dwelt there permanently—to a bedroom, where a man was waiting for us in the doorway. A pleasant-looking fellow in early middle age, balding, a little moustache. He was wearing a sweater over a shirt and tie and it made him look younger. This man was a doctor—I can't recall his name—but he had interviewed Gabriel on his previous trip. We all shook hands, Adam introducing me as Gabriel's oldest friend. The bedroom had been recently decorated and the smell of the new off-white paint lingered. There was a bed and a dresser, three chairs; a window overlooked a small yard and a chain-link fence to the parking lot of what looked like one of the technology companies that you saw everywhere in that part of Zurich West.

It all seemed awkward at first, at least for the three of us, but like many Swiss, the doctor spoke excellent English, and he asked Gabriel if he was absolutely certain that this was the course he wished to pursue. We were all standing around him at that point and Gabriel looked far from pleased by the attention.

"Yes, yes, let's get on with it, for Christ's sake."

The doctor went over to the dresser and returned with a small plastic cup.

"This is a sedative, Mr. Fontaine. It will relax you. In a few minutes you'll begin to feel sleepy. I think it's probably best if you lie down after you drink this."

"Let's do that right now, Adam," Gabriel said.

Adam nodded and turned the wheelchair around, drawing it back alongside the bed. Then he carefully lifted the old man onto the bed and put a pillow behind him, covered his legs with a blanket.

"All right," Gabriel said. "I'll take that stuff now." And he drank the sedative quickly.

Adam had leaned forward and was whispering, but we could all hear him, even the nurse who was standing by the doorway.

"Are you sure about this, sir?" he asked. "There's still time. We can go back to the hotel and take a plane home. Just say the word."

But Gabriel was shaking his head. "No, no, this is what I want. We stick to the plan." He lay there propped against the pillow, frowning and silent. The doctor came over to the bed with another plastic cup.

"Mr. Fontaine, I want you to drink this now. You'll find it a little bitter, but it'll settle things down inside. Keep you from regurgitating."

Gabriel drank it and made a face. "Jesus, that's awful stuff," he said, staring up at the white ceiling.

I was standing by the window looking out at the sunlit morning. Beyond the fence in the parking lot at the rear of the building on the next street, a woman carrying a briefcase or computer bag was walking to her car. I watched her place the bag on the back seat and then get in and drive away. Only a week earlier I had been at Woolford Abbey. Susan and I had talked long into the night, and the next morning she was up before me. I heard her getting ready for work, padding bare-foot along the hallway, running bathwater. Just as she used to do as a teenager. Downstairs a radio was playing. One of Bach's orchestral suites. The night before had been difficult in many ways, and now I felt we needed a rest from each other. A chance to gather strength to get through the next few days. I'm sure Susan felt exactly the same. Before she left, how-ever, she looked in through the doorway of my bedroom. At least I heard her pause there, for I had closed my eyes. Then I heard her footsteps on the stairs—she was wearing shoes by then—and a moment later the radio was turned off and a door closed.

When I went down to make my breakfast, I saw the note on the kitchen counter. She hoped I could find my way around the school and amuse myself for the day. She men-tioned the Farloe Library. Told me to introduce myself to somebody or other. She also said she was going to make a res-ervation for dinner at a little French restaurant in the village for Wednesday night. The place was new and very popular, so she had to book early.

Amid these musings, I'd hardly noticed that Adam had pulled a chair to the side of the bed and was now holding Gabriel's hand, and I thought how fortunate Gabriel was to have this young man with him at the end. To be truthful, I myself felt a bit superfluous in that bedroom.

I heard the doctor say, "I think you're ready now, Mr. Fontaine," and Gabriel replied, "I'm ready now, Doc. Anytime." His voice was drowsy but the intonation, the American slang, still reminded me of a youthful Gabriel.

With Adam now sitting beside him, I couldn't see Gabriel's face, just his legs covered by the blanket. Then the doctor was by the bed with a tray upon which was a glass of water and something else—the pills, I suppose. I found myself glancing at the nurse who was standing by the dresser, and she looked directly at me and nodded sympathetically. When the doctor left the bedside, I went over to Gabriel; he was sitting up to finish the pills with the last of the water. Then Adam settled his head against the pillow. Gabriel seemed not to see me. His look was unfocused, far away, but after a moment he said, "Roll me on my side, Adam, I want to be on my side." Adam turned him towards the wall, and so Gabriel's back was to us, but I heard his voice, though only faintly. "So long there, James."

It was almost as if for a while he'd forgotten I was there, and it reminded me of other times in his room at the St. Lawrence Hotel when he'd grown tired of my company and wheeled himself over to the giant jigsaw puzzle, there to sit moodily fitting together pieces of the sky or sea, while I quietly opened the door and left.

He died in his sleep—in a matter of minutes—and I took a taxi back to the hotel.

Adam had many things to do: the coroner and the police had been called, just routine apparently; arrangements had to be made for Gabriel's cremation and the transport of his ashes back to the States. There were many papers to sign. We agreed to meet for a drink at five that afternoon. What did I do with the rest of that Monday? I wandered about the city, going into bookshops and austere old Protestant churches. I walked by the river and returned to the hotel for lunch. I had two glasses of wine with the meal and afterwards a nap in my room. I had watched a man I once knew as a boy take his own life and die peacefully as he had wished, and I was glad that I had come along to Zurich to be with him.

At five o'clock I went up to the suite and Adam greeted me at the door. I could see that I had interrupted a phone call, and he gestured towards a chair as he went back across the room to the telephone. Adam seemed more relaxed now in slacks and sweater, his job nearly done. I sat listening while he talked to his friend in Boston, and I couldn't help noticing the warmth and affection in his voice. Afterwards he opened a bottle of champagne and surprised me by taking a glass himself.

"Just one now and then," he said, adding, "I'd like to propose a toast to the memory of Gabriel Fontaine."

Strange, I thought, this evident loyalty to a man who in the course of a day must have insulted Adam Trench a dozen times. Yet for all I knew, Gabriel may have left him all his money, and Adam was now a rich man. In such circumstances, who would not toast his benefactor? As for me, I had decidedly mixed feelings about Gabriel Fontaine, but nevertheless raised my glass.

I think we both felt uncomfortable after that, two timid strangers in another country, thrown together under the influence of a powerful third party. And now with that party's absence? Well, as I've said, it was uncomfortable, and I was glad that neither of us had suggested dinner, for I'm sure we both would have agreed and then have had an awkward evening. To paper over the cracks that afternoon, Adam talked about his friend Donald Petty and how they were looking forward to meeting on Wednesday afternoon. Adam told me that each visit now to the Boston airport was special for them, a physical reminder of how fortunate they were still to be together. It seems that Donald had booked a seat on American Airlines Flight 11 for Los Angeles on September 11, 2001, a flight, of course, that ended at the North Tower of the World Trade Center. He had been going out to look at a private collection, quite a good one apparently, owned by the wealthy widow of a movie producer. This woman used to live in Boston and knew Donald's family. But the day after she invited him to come out, she phoned back to say she'd changed her mind, and by so doing, his life was spared. After the 9/11 calamity, the FBI naturally were interested in Donald Petty's cancelled reservation, and visited his gallery and their apartment. Alan and Donald both came under intense scrutiny for a while. A difficult time. But the authorities were finally satisfied that it was nothing more than an innocent change in plans. September 11, then, was a special day for them and Logan Airport a special place. Whenever they arrived or departed, they now held hands and remembered. I had another glass of champagne while I listened to Adam's story, a hymn to dumb luck. Then it was time to go.

We did, however, exchange addresses and promise to keep in touch. Why do we say these things when we don't really mean them? I did send him a Christmas card that year and received one back late in January. Adam wrote that he and Donald had been in Hawaii for the holidays and he was only now catching up on his mail. He wished me a happy 2005. The next year neither of us bothered.

There was to be an *outing*. This quaint word was introduced at the breakfast table by my uncle. This was the
morning after Odette told me her news, and I was tired
and cranky. To use one of Mrs. Moore's expressions, I had a
"face on me," the face of someone determined to punish evil-
doers wherever he found them, the face of a fourteen-year-old
version of some fanatical reformer, Oliver Cromwell perhaps.
I intended to ignore Odette's warnings and tell Gabriel that he
had duties to perform.

At the breakfast table, Uncle Chester looked over his paper
and told me we'd been invited on an outing; we were going
that afternoon on a tourist boat around Bonaventure Island
to look at the millions of seabirds that bred and nested there.
Everyone was leaving next Saturday, he said, and they wanted
to see the birds before they returned home. As for him, he
had been around the island years before, and if it came to
that, he wasn't much interested in birds; nevertheless, he was
indulging friends, and so would I please adjust my features

into something approaching amiability; it was, he said, unbe-
coming in a healthy boy to look so grim on a sunny morning
when good things lay in the offing. Another of his words, *offing*,
the pretentious old bugger. I say old, for so he seemed at the
time, though it occurs to me that he was then about the same
age as my own son is now.

Later we set off in the Willys, my uncle humming a tune,
and it's odd but I've just remembered its long-buried name.
"The Whistler and His Dog." As a small child in the 1930s, I used
to hear it on the radio played by a military band. Quite possibly it was the introductory theme to a newscast, for I seem to
remember my father listening by the radio to the six o'clock
news before sitting down to his dinner. You seldom hear such
tunes nowadays; they conjure up spats and those lamps with
tasselled shades that cast a narrow yellow light. Like the one
in my mother's bedroom under which she read the novels
of Ellen Glasgow and A.J. Cronin. Now and then I hear "The
Whistler and His Dog" on a program of light music on the
CBC played by the Bournemouth Symphony Orchestra. And
it never fails to produce a prickling along the back of my neck,
a palpable intimation of unrecoverable time and its accompanying sadness, the very impulse that inspired Alfred T's lyrical
masterpiece "Tears, Idle Tears."

Gabriel was delighted to see me and even my sombre coun-
tenance didn't faze him. Perhaps by then he was used to vari-
ations of it, though he'd been drinking that day and this may
have accounted for his tolerance of my glum humour. He told
me he didn't give a damn about the birds, but it would be a
change of scenery. He had dressed for the occasion in a blue

blazer and white ducks. He even had a white yachtsman's cap. I wanted to pretend that he looked silly in this getup, but I knew he didn't; he looked in fact outrageously handsome. He told me we were running late; the mater had just phoned from the lounge and was anxious to be on her way. It didn't seem the right time to inform him of his nascent fatherhood.

As I pushed him along the hallway, we saw Odette coming out of a room stuffing used sheets into a hamper on the little trolley she wheeled from door to door. She smiled as we approached. From the open doorway, another girl was making the bed. It wasn't Pauline, who, I learned later, had been fired for stealing. She'd been caught taking home those little bars of hotel soap. Gabriel told Odette about our excursion and she wished us a good time, and after looking both ways down the hall, she leaned over and kissed Gabriel on both cheeks. She kissed me too, though only the one time, and said, "When you get near the island, don't open your mouth when you look up." Gabriel had a good laugh at that, and I must have offered a smile too, wondering at the same time how she could be so cheerful in the face of all that was happening to her. But what did I know of the heart's affections? Gabriel, it seemed, could do no wrong and that was that. As I opened the door leading to the service elevator, I saw her with towels in one arm. She was waving to us with the other.

The boat held perhaps thirty passengers, two-thirds of whom could sit inside behind windows. The rest of us chose the open air in the stern. That seemed like a good idea when we set out and the sun was shining. But the sky was filling with clouds as we headed seaward. I think we were the only English-speaking people aboard. There were a half dozen priests in their soutanes, and they were having the time of their lives, led by a big fellow with a noisy laugh, the kind of priest—perhaps it's old movies that do this to us—you could picture standing at home plate during recess at a parochial school, hitting fly balls to outfielders. Showing the boys how it was done. I noticed how deferential the women were towards these black-clad holy men, offering them window seats, making way for them and their little Brownie cameras. The women cast shy glances our way too. We were Americans staying at the big hotel, denizens of a magical land, home of Coca-Cola and baseball and Technicolor movies. We were exotic creatures, the envy of the world and at ease anywhere in it. America's stock was never higher than during that final year of the Second World War when the U.S.A. was saving us all from Hitler and Tojo. I must have felt a pang of disloyalty that afternoon as I basked in the envious looks of those French-Canadian tourists.

Mrs. F had brought along a Thermos of cocktails, and Gabriel, whose wheelchair had been eased down a little ramp by a deckhand into the open area at the rear of the boat, told me that he wished he had something to put into our Cokes. But he could do nothing about it; his friend in the bar had told him it was near the end of the month and the hotel's liquor ration was low. The man didn't feel he could take the risk. They'd had a conversation about it that morning in the corridor by the service elevator. Gabriel, however, suspected that his mother was behind it all. He believed that she'd discovered his source and had threatened to tell the man's employer. It infuriated him to watch his mother seated against the

lurch of the boat, filling Dixie cups held by my uncle and the
Porters. Eleanor Fontaine looked her usual glamorous self
that afternoon in her slacks and sweater, a kerchief knotted
beneath her chin. Large dark glasses. Uncle Chester and Mr.
Porter were having a mild argument over the definition of
the word *launch* and whether the term could accurately be
used to describe the vessel we were on at the time. Now and
then an unpleasant look crossed my uncle's face, a sure sign
of his mounting impatience with Sam Porter. With all of us,
I imagine. There were two pretty sisters about my age. They
were with their parents and they kept looking back at Gabriel.
He had taken off the yachtsman's cap before the wind could
snatch it away, something I had hoped to see, for that would
surely have ruffled his carefully managed *amour-propre*. But no
such luck. And now his dark Tyrone Power hair, unloosed by
the wind, made him even more mysteriously attractive. How
I hated him that afternoon!

Rounding the island, we felt the direct force of the wind
as the boat plunged through the heaving, grey water, the bow
rising and falling, the spray catching us unawares. Without
our having noticed it, the sun had disappeared for the day,
and everything seemed suddenly gloomy and forbidding.
The captain was talking in French about the various kinds of
birds, but no one seemed to be listening, the rise and fall of
the boat commanding our attention. Only the jolly priests
seemed to be enjoying the excursion, and they took it upon
themselves to cheer the rest of us up. With each lurch of
the boat, they sang out a French version of "Whoops-a-Daisy"

and laughed. There was naturally the inevitable queasiness among some, and a few came back to be sick over the side. The air was filled with the cries of seabirds as they soared above us in the grey windy sky. I watched the gannets dive-bombing into the sea like miniature Stukas. Along the outer cliffside of the island, millions of birds were nesting and feeding and squawking. Avian life in all its fecundity. I chose that moment beneath the cliffs of Bonaventure Island with that terrible bird racket and the wind and the shit-filled sky (Odette was right) to tell Gabriel.

My lips were next to his ear and tousled hair. He was ignoring the birds, gazing through his binoculars out to sea.

"She's pregnant, you know," I said.

He didn't miss a beat, kept scanning the grey horizon. "What's that, old boy?" His Ronald Colman accent.

"Odette's going to have a baby," I said. "She's only fifteen, Gabriel, for God's sake."

He began to talk, incredibly enough, about a German submarine and the possibility of being torpedoed. "Imagine a U-boat, James," he said. "Somewhere out there. It's Sunday afternoon and the crew has been bored for weeks. No action at all. Then the captain sights us through his periscope and decides to send us under. Give the crew some battle station practice. Cheer them up to hit something. Good for morale and all that. Heil Hitler, boys."

He put down the binoculars and smiled at me. The wind was giving us a terrible buffeting, pressing itself in bursts against our faces.

"Think of it, James," Gabriel shouted. A few people briefly looked our way. "Suppose we could see it coming, its nasty-looking snout just under the surface. Over there, say." He pointed, and stupidly I looked. "Here it comes, by God," he said. "We're going to be blown to pieces in the next few seconds. There's nothing we can do about it. No more future. No more anything. And then . . ." He was looking through the glasses again. "Pieces of us in the water for these goddamn seagulls. And it would be in all the newspapers. On the radio. Maybe even *The March of Time*. They'd fly a crew down here to take pictures of the wreckage. People would see it in movie theatres from Boston to San Francisco."

I was going to bring up Odette's name again, but Gabriel's mother came over and fell sideways against me on the seat, grasping my arm and laughing. The ends of her kerchief were flapping madly in the wind. She was a little tight.

"Isn't this fun, boys?" she cried. She was squeezing my arm, holding on against the sway of the boat.

"Yes, Mother," Gabriel said. "It's fun, fun, fun. But I was just telling James here about the possibility of us being blown up by a German torpedo."

"Don't be silly, Gabriel," she said. "We're enjoying ourselves. Having a lovely time, and you can only think of unpleasant things."

"Unpleasant things are a part of life, Mommy," he said, still peering through the binoculars. "You must have learned that by now."

"Listen to what I have to put up with, James," Mrs. Fontaine said. "I hope you're not as saucy to your mother."

"James would never be saucy to his mother," said Gabriel. "James is a good boy. I, on the other hand, am a bad boy."

I wanted to knock those goddamn binoculars out of his hands. "Have another drink, Mother," Gabriel said.

Mrs. Fontaine got up, leaning against me for a moment. "Oh, go to hell, you selfish little . . ."

I didn't catch the noun; it was carried off by the wind as she made her way back to the Porters and my uncle.

By then we had passed the other end of the island and turned landward, the wind behind us now as we surged forward. People's spirits lifted. The big, loud priest was telling a story that was making everyone in the cabin laugh. Gabriel had put away the binoculars and settled the yachtsman's cap on his head once again. He was trailing a hand over the side of the boat and humming something familiar, a show tune we must have listened to in his room. I wanted to talk about Odette, but I didn't. Perhaps by then I felt I had done my duty, at least, in mentioning her condition, though that may not be the entire truth. The entire truth may have more to do with my cowardly streak, my unwillingness to confront him.

By the end of the afternoon, I think we all agreed that the outing had been a disappointment. As for me, I intended never to speak to Gabriel Fontaine again, and for the rest of that week I resolutely stayed away from the St. Lawrence Hotel. By now my uncle was so resigned to my fits of obdurate moodiness that each afternoon he went to Percé alone and without comment. That is, until Saturday when he told me (I remember we were standing in the hallway after lunch, each of us, by a stroke of unfortunate timing, about to ascend the stairs) that

I might at the very least have the civility to say goodbye to people (guests in our country) whom we had known all summer. Not to do so was a reflection on manners and breeding, a stain on the family's honour. Well, I'm exaggerating. He didn't quite say that, but I got the message anyway and went with him.

They were leaving on the afternoon train, and when we got there, the luggage was already on the front veranda of the hotel. The taxi was waiting, and the dour Emile was carrying the bags to his Ford truck. Uncle Chester was filled with the bonhomie of the host who at last can count on the departure of guests who have been from time to time unduly wearisome. There were hugs and kisses and promises to keep in touch.

"What a divine summer it has been, James," said Mrs. F, holding me to her richly scented blouse. "Thank you so much for being Gabriel's friend."

My periodic absences over the summer seemed not to have tarnished her image of me as her son's loyal friend, though perhaps Eleanor Fontaine didn't mean a word of what she said and never had.

Gabriel was already in the taxi. He knew I was angry with him and why, and that's all that mattered to me. He had rolled the window down and was looking out at me, smiling.

"So long, pal," he said. "Don't take any wooden nickels." A dopey catchphrase of the day.

We didn't shake hands. I turned instead to watch Emile fit the wheelchair into the back of the truck and lock the tailgate. And they were on their way, with some of the hotel staff waving goodbye from the veranda.

I wondered then what Gabriel and Odette had said to each other on this last morning.

Later she told me that he'd promised to write. Not for a moment did I believe that he ever would, but at least I had the sense not to say as much. This was on our last walk, on the Monday evening before I left. We were crossing the railway bridge towards the beach on the seaward side of the bar, but halfway across, Odette stopped and told me she didn't feel like a long walk. So we leaned against the railing and watched the incoming tide as it flowed beneath us, rocking the fishing boats moored against the wharf. It was a still, grey evening, but over the mountains there were flaring, pale flashes of light behind the clouds. It looked theatrical, but we both felt nervous, city kids after all and still leery of country weather, unable to read the wind and the sky.

Odette told me her father too was taking the train the next day and this bothered me, though I didn't let on. The truth is, I had been looking forward to the coziness of my compartment with only the last hundred pages of *Great Expectations* for company. It was all I needed to get me to Toronto. I didn't want to sit up all the way to Montreal answering Olivier Huard's questions about life in Ontario. Odette told me how fed up her father was with the way things were going in Quebec. In early August there had been a provincial election, and the right-wing Union Nationale under Maurice Duplessis had won convincingly. You could still see some of the candidates' posters nailed on trees and hydro poles. According to Odette's father, it was a victory for the Church. The priests would now be advising the politicians. Fascists all of them, and thick as thieves, he said. So I would have to listen to all that as well. If I didn't, he would likely consider me just another privileged English brat hiding away in a private compartment paid for by his rich father. Why I should have worried about what Olivier Huard thought of me is a good question, but I have no answer.

On that last evening Odette was uncommonly quiet, and I too fell silent as we watched those inflamed clouds across the mountains. I hadn't expected her old familiar self—cheerfully combative and curious—no, she had a great many things on her mind and I understood that. Still, this was different. It seemed Gabriel's departure had left Odette and me suddenly and peculiarly estranged from each other. As though Gabriel had been the star in our little planetary system, holding us both firmly in orbit around him. And with his departure we were cast adrift, strangers once again. I can see all that now, but I suspect that on the railway bridge that evening, I was merely hurt.

I had money for her in an envelope. I had taken an envelope from the secretary in the front hallway that morning while Mrs. Moore was out and Uncle Chester's Smith Corona was clacking away upstairs. The envelope smelled faintly of potpourri, an old woman's smell. I waited until we were off the bridge lest the envelope fall between our hands. I could imagine the despair in watching it flutter through the railway ties to the fast-moving water below. On the pathway back to the village I handed it to her, a small white rectangle in the darkness between us.

"Here," I said.

She stopped. "What's this?"

"It's twenty-five dollars," I said. "It's all I have." The last phrase was pathetic and I knew that the minute I said it. And what did I expect from her anyway? Was I waiting for her to throw her arms around me and weep in gratitude? Probably I was, though I knew very well that it wasn't Odette's style. Yet I was disappointed when she gave me only a perfunctory hug and said, "Thanks, James. You're a good guy."

We didn't linger by the side of her house. The storm was now rumbling into the distance, heading out to sea, but it had started to rain and so we hastily said goodbye and I sprinted across the field. I think I was in tears as I ran, and I know that I behaved badly when I got to the house. My uncle and Mrs. Moore were at the dining-room table talking, watching the storm move southward towards Percé. They were drinking tea and eating buns freshly baked by Mrs. Moore *for me*. A treat on my last night in her house. Of course, they expected me to join them, but I curtly refused and disappeared up the stairs to my room. How we puzzle and disappoint our elders when we are young. Transfer our damaged feelings into behaviour that is hurtful and makes no sense to those who wish us well. This was something I would learn on evenings many years later, when other doors slammed and I was left to stare at the walls.

That night I lay awake a long time and so I slept through Odette's walk down the lane to the highway and the arrival of the little truck that would take her to the St. Lawrence Hotel. It was the only morning of the entire summer that I missed seeing her, and over the years I have come to regard my sleeping in that day as an act of disloyalty to love itself.

233

I expected a surly response at the breakfast table and felt I deserved it. But all was sweetness and light, my uncle brimming with good humour, and Mrs. Moore urging me to have bacon and eggs, a dish usually reserved for Sunday lunch. What good, forgiving people they really were, I thought. Or were they just happy to see the last of me? In any case, to please Mrs. Moore I ate several of her buns, too many in fact, for I remember feeling quite plugged for a while that morning. Later Uncle Chester drove me to the station and wished me well in my second year at Groveland, reminding me to pass on greetings to old colleagues. I assured him that I would, though I never did. He also told me to say hello for him to my mother and Aunt Margery, pointedly excluding my father in his salutations, and I wasn't surprised. I knew J. T. and Uncle Chester didn't really like each other. Finally my uncle supposed that we'd all be together again for a jolly time at Christmas, and naturally I agreed. I see him even now as I did from that train window, waving goodbye before turning to walk briskly towards the blue Willys, a trim man with a little sandy moustache, slightly effeminate in manner, wearing tan trousers with a white tennis sweater thrown across the back of his shirt and knotted at the throat.

Watching him drive away I was glad to be alone at last, though I was anxious too as I looked around for Odette's father. Wondering how I could avoid him. Would he seek me out? Knock on the door and invite himself in for a chat? Somehow he struck me as a man who was capable of doing exactly that. Yet only two or three other people got on the train that afternoon, and soon the bell began to ring, and with a short blast of the whistle, we were moving. And no Olivier Huard aboard. It was selfish, but I felt inexpressible relief at the prospect of the journey ahead, alone with my novel. As we slowly passed over the bridge onto the bar, I looked across the river to the village. Soon I could see Mrs. Moore's house with washing on the line. She had already cleaned my aerie, and those towels and sheets and blankets that had been mine for the summer would soon be ironed and put away. My room would now be as bare as a monk's cell. In front of the Huards' house, the children too young for school were running about the yard with the black-and-white collie. Odette would soon be finishing her day's work at the hotel. But where was her father? Why was he not on the train returning to Montreal and his job in the munitions factory? Had Odette told her parents about her pregnancy and were they even now sitting at the kitchen table discussing what to do? Perhaps Olivier Huard was completely discouraged by such news coming from his oldest child, his favourite. Maybe he had drunk too much beer and was now lying on a bed in his clothes, afraid to get up.

I wondered too what Gabriel was doing just then. Imagined him with his mother, shopping for clothes in a fancy store in Boston. Shirts and sweaters and ties piled on a counter. Jackets and a new blazer on wooden hangers. Black oxfords with shoe trees in them. Perhaps his father was home from Washington for a few days. He would drive Gabriel down to his school, and on the way they would have lunch at a country inn, just as my parents and I would en route to Groveland later in the week. I saw Gabriel in the dining room of that inn opening a package, a gift from his father. A gold-plated pen and pencil set. Or cufflinks with matching tie bar in a blue box with satin lining. "Gee, Dad, that's swell. Thanks a lot." And all the time wishing he could have a glass of wine like his parents. But all this was only in my imagination. What did I really know? At school the masters always talked of solving problems, finding answers. It was always about answers. But what if many things we encounter have no answers? What if they just remain unsolved mysteries? Why for instance had my mother's nerves failed her? How could you like a person yet not like him too? How could I still have such strong feelings for a girl I now realized I didn't know all that well? And what was going to become of her? And why did I still care so much?

So many things then seemed indeterminate, stories without endings. And looking out the train window on that late-summer afternoon in my fifteenth year, I think I sensed, in a small way at least, that such mysteries lay at the heart of everything that would matter in my life.

ENVOI

My daughter died nearly a year after Gabriel. She had returned to Toronto in January with Sophie Wasserman. At first Susan reluctantly agreed to continue with the chemotherapy she had begun at the Churchill Hospital in Headington, but after a few weeks she refused further treatment. Said it only made her feel more miserable, and she challenged the oncologist to prove that it would do anything more than prolong her existence by a few more months. I gather he didn't argue too strenuously with her decision. We moved her to a hospice where the people could not have been kinder. Susan knew she was dying, and I think what bothered her as much as that brutal fact and the accompanying pain was the humiliation of it all. Cancer is such a wasting disease; day by day it reduces its victim to a haggard caricature of her former self. As the weeks passed, I could see how Susan was beginning to look like her mother, and this brought to mind an evening more than twenty years earlier, when Leah had grasped my hand as I was leaving and whispered, "Try to remember me as I was before this." Useless to point out how none of that matters, because, of course, to some it does. To some, being pitied is almost as unbearable as the disease itself.

A couple of months before the end, Susan told me it wasn't necessary to visit so often. I had been seeing her every after-noon because I wanted to, but also because I had the time. The others—Brenda and the children, David and Nikki, and Sophie—usually came by during the evening hours. But Susan told me that two or three times a week would be fine. She didn't talk about her pain, just mentioned the enormous fatigue, but I could tell she was embarrassed to look and feel so ill.

One day I decided to tell her the truth about my trip to Zurich with Adam Trench and Gabriel. It was a humid after-noon in late August, and I remember the tinny racket of the air conditioner, which must have been old. Beyond the window a soiled grey sky, and on the street below, the roofs of passing cars and people walking. The other patient in the room, a woman even younger than Susan, had fallen into her morphine sleep while watching a television serial. The program was still on but muted, the actors soundlessly talking, gesturing, weeping. As she listened to me, Susan sipped water from a glass straw with its little elbow. I described Gabriel's condition and the young man who was looking after him, and the bungalow with its chain-link fence and the parking lot. I told her about the nurse and the doctor and how Gabriel died. I apologized for not tell-ing the truth before, but at the time the news of her disease was still so raw that I didn't want to upset her further. Susan put down the glass and smiled. Squeezed my hand and told me she wanted to sleep.

In my apartment I worried about what I had said, for I didn't want her to think that I was encouraging her to do anything that she didn't want to do. Yet I was riven by her suffering. How long would it last, and was it necessary? I couldn't help thinking of Gabriel's death, which had seemed to me so peaceful and sane. That night I looked up Web sites on assisted suicide, taking notes and drinking too much whisky. But over the next few visits, Susan said nothing about it, and I thought she'd dismissed the idea outright.

Then, about two weeks later, she mentioned it. She was muddled that day—I suspect they had adjusted her pain medication—and she said, "That Swiss thing you talked about yesterday, Dad? With your friend?"

"Yes?"

"If those people were down the street, I'd go in a minute. But Europe? The plane ride? All that hassle?" She allowed herself a small, mirthless laugh. "I guess I'm just too tired to die."

Six weeks later she was dead, and we buried her in Mount Pleasant Cemetery, not all that far from the graves of my parents and Aunt Margery and Uncle Chester, distant ghosts, awakened briefly by my chance encounter with Gabriel Fontaine in front of a London hotel one afternoon in October.